UNFINISHED
WORLD

OTHER WORK BY
JOHN OLSON

POETRY

Weave of the Dream King (2021)
Dada Budapest (2017)
Larynx Galaxy (2012)
Backscatter: New and Selected Poems (2008)
The Night I Dropped Shakespeare on the Cat (2006)
Oxbow Kazoo (2005)
Free Stream Velocity (2003)
Echo Regime (2000)
Logo Lagoon (1999)
Eggs & Mirrors (1999)
Swarm of Edges (1996)

FICTION

You Know There's Something (2023)
Mingled Yarn (2020)
In Advance of the Broken Justy (2016)
The Seeing Machine (2012)
The Nothing That Is (2010)
Souls of Wind (2008)

UNFINISHED WORLD

A NOVEL BY

JOHN OLSON

QUALE PRESS

ISBN: 978-1-935835-37-0
LCCN: 2025942808

Front Cover: *Primer for a New Topography*,
by Peggy Murphy, acrylic painting 36" x 36"

Back Cover: *The Monkey Pod Tree*,
digital photograph by John Olson

Quale Press

www.quale.com

For Roberta

Existence is a series of footnotes to a vast, obscure, unfinished masterpiece.
—Vladimir Nabokov

As-tu senti parfois que rien ne finissait?
Et qu'on soit là ou pas, quand même, on y serait

Have you sometimes felt that nothing finishes?
And that whether one is there or not, we would still be there
—Dominique A

There are things I have left undone. I never wrote the Great American Novel. But I tried. I never read all of Hegel. Did I intend to read all of Hegel? I never learned to play the guitar. I never met Bob Dylan. I never bungee jumped from the Empire State Building. Which is a good thing. This is nothing I intended. Not doing something unintended is not entirely reliable. There are a lot of things I did that I didn't mean to do. I never meant to hurt you, whoever you are, wherever you are. I'm sorry. I never became a lawyer. I never visited another planet. I never shook hands with a high French official in the Hall of Mirrors at Versailles. There are some things I did, of which I am glad. I rode a calico horse in Pacific surf. I guarded Jane Fonda's luggage by an airport phone booth. I married a kind and beautiful woman. I carried water and chopped wood. And as I approached the end of my days I discovered there was a lot more to it I hadn't yet finished doing.

The closer I get to the end of my life, the more it feels like dead friends. Dead parents. Dead brother. Dead ambitions. Dead ecologies. Dead batteries. So I go back in time and undo what I did and do what I should've done and don't do what I shouldn't have done. I say what I should've said and unsay what I shouldn't have said. And this goes on all day and into the night until sleep and unconsciousness give me some relief. Day after day. Ad nauseum. And then there's laundry. Bedsheets and towels. Socks and underwear. Ghosts and ghostly ideas. Metal tongs. Ectoplasmic tongues. It always seems like the air is hiding something. You can feel something there. Like Peter Falk in *Wings of Desire* feeling the angel nearby. I can't see you. But I know you're there.

How much experience fits within the parameters of reason? Half? Three-quarters? Most of the time we're blind as worms in empirical dirt. Bedraggled, goofily morose, potato chips on the coffee table. Most of life is a mantra of dishevelment. When was the last time you felt like robbing a jewelry store? There's nobody here but introspection. It's time all this protocol meant something besides encouragement, or a back rub. I think it's time we start talking about Umwelt. Otherwise, everything is everywhere. Nothing matters as much as nothingness. In this scenario, Percy Bysshe Shelley isn't dead. He's sleeping like oil on the wrist of Prometheus. We see the sparkle of consciousness and go to the mountains, awed by the medicine we took. It did something. It let the ghosts in. Tent poles made it plausible. Olivier Messiaen made it audible.

In 1942, thousands of copies of Paul Éluard's poem "Liberté" were dropped by parachute by British aircraft of the Royal Air Force above occupied France. Poetry as rain. As lightning. As paper fluttering down through a hail of bullets.

In 1518, the citizens of Strasbourg began dancing frenziedly and uncontrollably for a period of about two months before coming to a stop. No one had an explanation for the behavior. The most widely accepted theory is that of medical historian John Waller, who surmised that the dancing plague, as it came to be known, was a form of mass psychogenic disorder, and that such outbreaks are often a response to extreme stress.

In May 2001, reports began spreading in New Delhi, India, about a monkey-like creature appearing at night and attacking people. Eyewitness accounts were often inconsistent, but tended to describe the creature as about four feet tall, covered in thick black hair, with a metal helmet, metal claws, glowing red eyes and three buttons on its chest. Some reports also claim that the monkey-man wore roller skates. I love the idea of a mad-monkey on roller skates, with three buttons on his chest. Why three? Why not a zipper? Cue "Monkey Man," by The Rolling Stones.

Horizons have always fascinated me. I can stare at them forever. Horizons are all about forever. It's what they do. They reveal a never-ending arrival for a forever-receding destination. It's where the future resides. The future never arrives. As soon as the future arrives, it ceases being the future and becomes the present, which is here for a second, if that, and then it becomes the past, which is huge, and full of catacombs and labyrinths, weird juxtapositions and dramas staged in cars with frosted windshields and stinky heaters. Bullets ricocheting off prairie rocks. Musty smell of magazines in a deserted house. Salutes to the American flag which always felt odd and unrelated to the principles of learning. I always wondered why it was invisible under a God who was also invisible. Horizons always seem so promising. And then they become motels. And TV.

There is a prison outside the Estonian village of Rummu which is now submerged in a lake. People like to visit the beaches below which the prison sleeps in crystal clear water. They find it fun to dive and swim between its walls and feed their curiosity the sinister passages through which they glide with happy buoyancy. What surprises me is how the prison has solidly resisted any transformative appearance. It is still very much a prison. Everything about it seems brutal and cruel and calculated to kill the spirit. I find prisons fascinating, though I've only been in one once as a visitor. When I left, even though I'd only been behind bars for several hours, the world was exquisite in its detail. The worse prisons aren't made of iron or stone, but the ones that grow in you imperceptibly like coral. You don't even know it's there, until you try to come up for air.

Music always seems to be searching for something, even when it just seems to be wandering around in space, or entertaining grocery shoppers. I saw a symphony once disguised as a cluster of ferns in a forest of words and said to myself it takes a lot to make a sound extend itself across the desolations of modern life. You need a lot of geometry and towels. D minor on a Fender Stratocaster, squeaky bedsprings, ionized arias, and jingly implications. How many drugs does the body manufacture? Enough to function. How many drugs does an individual require to commune with the universe? Depends. Sometimes the moment calls for Duende. Sometimes Baton Rouge. Life can be rigid as a stripper pole. But given the right music, it can bend.

The attraction to the intangible is both easy and hard to explain. Easy because the intangible doesn't cost a dime. It's free. That's why it's hard. Hard to value. Hard to explain. The intangible won't get you to work on time, adorn your body, or appease an appetite. The intangible is intractable, but actual. Because nothing is nothing without something to make it nothing.

Some things in life are achieved through chicanery. Swelling, bloating, turgescence. All of it an act, of course, a representation possessed of sabotage and sackcloth calculated to arouse esteem and opportunity in the eyes of the pious. I think you know where this is going. If your answer is the latrine, I salute you. We can laugh now, and relax. No, this isn't a survey, it's more like a filiation mulled in balderdash with a dollop of bunkum and a side order of flapdoodle. These things come in handy when you're attempting to swagger across the barroom floor with your spurs jingling and your conjectures lagging behind like a three-legged dog. And don't you know that literature has gone the way of the deadlight? If you've spent any time at all eavesdropping on Kerouac's letters, you'll know there's a place for ecstasy, and is revealed to you by flashlight.

If you see a mountain in the distance, don't rush towards it. Let it come to you. Point a stampede at it, of words and definitions. Write things down. It is with pleasure that I splash the notation with nouns. The immense sleet that blew it there continued its journey north. I felt within me a feeling of humble beginnings develop into a story. I was somewhere south of lethargy coming to in a bar in the Black Forest of Germany. I could hear a gust of wind outside, and injustice and clamors of deification. A flash of lightning as The Elves of Redemption thundered across the bridge. It has always been such. Some people want to know what. Others want to know why. I want to know what distant green knowledge is harbored in the skull and why it's so hard to find.

Nothing ever gets done around here. And why should it? We're a nuclear people. We recline in chairs and stare out the window believing that there's a world there. With people in it. And hemoglobin and dogs. Perceptions don't just see things. Smell things. Feel things. They create things. Break an egg and you get a blob of gold in a goo of albumin. This is our morning allegory. But don't make the same mistake I did. Go around forever interpreting things. Looking for omens. Forget the scenery. Let's get ontic. Let's lean back and get hypnopompic. Sometimes it takes an earthquake to write an editorial and a pair of bad shoes to do justice to a good dance.

It wasn't really a choice. I suck at following instructions. Words are a different story. Because I don't know. We're all alone. The world is by your side, but it's busy stabbing the bureau with harsh afternoon light. I know what to do. Hold this sentence a minute while I get all sparkly and serious. Life is its own damn meaning. Our experiences are generally about something, and this one smells like sunset on the Ganges. Atman, Dharma, bubbles winking in sunlight. Existence tastes quick, like the wink of a wildcat. I sometimes wonder if I know what it is I'm saying. It all shoots out of my mouth in a spray of hummingbirds. It's a technocratic world. Somebody's got to be silly. And sometimes I just sit. The incentives are vicious. Humanity groans, overwhelmed by the future. Which doesn't exist. The important thing is to be so constantly ontological that people go out of their way to avoid you. Empathy comes later, with death and ice cream. It's a tough universe, and hard to accept. But if you do, you'll arrive at a meaning for everything.

There's an ancient church covered in ivy on the Normandy coast of France that fascinated Proust by its near invisibility due to the quantity of ivy obscuring it from view, and I believe he was also implying the paradox of language, that the more abundantly words are used to describe something, the more it disappears into unreality. Velocity speaks to me in the language of pure sensation. Is this the thunder of a divine presence? Let's just say the road is finally open. You'll have to run after it. But no hurry. It's better if things percolate. Drip slowly into consciousness. Welcome to my cave. Anxiety is a dashboard for the mouths of hell. Anger is an extrusion of bone. Shooting a gun is like drawing an underpass with an alcoholic crayon. Bang. I shot my mouth off again. It happens whenever there's a language around and the words are biting.

Generally, if I want to show a feeling, I take it out of my mouth and hang it in the air. The result is not always recognizable. Everything confuses me. Wrinkles play with the face, and a god hully gullies in my rug. Realizations come in the gravitational waves I attempt to surf. I don't understand everything about poker, or card games in general, but there are things about my past that drop into the water like propellers and drive things forward, causing remorse and logic to thrash about in strips of glittering metal. If I want to get rich, there are ways to do that. Art is different. It needs guts and hedonism. A spirit of joy. Convulsive beauty. Dead Sea mud settles to the bottom of the paragraph. And this is how the mind joins the quiet life of the refrigerator.

Does your life ever feel like an accident? Mine does. I'm not here of my own volition. I have little to say in the matter. The big decider here is destiny. And if the neocons get their wish for WWIII. This is how it's been my entire life. Tentative. Conditional. Uncertain. Things have always been iffy. Like some form of imposed Zen. Or Patsy Cline singing "Crazy" on the car CD player with a warm Texas breeze blowing through the open window of a pearl Silverado. There's a tornado forming in the distance. The engine's running hot. And you're not sure if this is the right road. That's when you hear the siren. It gets louder as it gets closer and whizzes by at ninety. The siren diminishes. Horses gallop across an open field. And the tornado has just touched down.

Follow me. I'll show you things. Big things. Little things. Weird things. The pain swimming beneath my face. The evolution of the T-shirt. The neuroses nibbling at the fringes of prose. The key to phenomena. The Baudelaire of apartment hunting. The history of Elvis's sneer. The fire in Rimbaud's eyes. Little Anthony's magnificent falsetto. When was the last time you fired a gun? Don't worry. This is the language of fog. I can make Rhode Island come out of my head whenever I try to explain anything. Music does this. I don't know what else to call it.

The problem is this: whoever I thought I was is you, all you, every atom. For every atom belonging to you as good belongs to the Bank of Warm Being. That's where you make your deposits of semen and DNA. We're all one happy family, we humans, we lumens, we aluminum catechumen, we constellations of bacteria flying the mind around like a helicopter.

Think of me as a window. I'll be your window. Nothing is wholly obvious without first being Terra Incognita. It therefore follows that syntax, and Shakespeare's beard, are equal to the task of popping in and out of the void like words spoken over the loudspeakers at the airport.

Who doesn't like showing off their scars? Each wound squints like an Icelandic saga. Each word is an organ of nerves. It walks out of the mouth teeming with daydreams. Blake's tiger prowling about two men on a muddy street. One of them is in despair. The other is on his way to the Stapleton International Airport outside Denver. It's your life, sisters and brothers. You go your way. I'll go mine. Tomorrow we'll rise early and sparkle like Polynesia. When the truth comes out, this will make a song. No one will be able to resist singing it. I do it quietly. And this is called writing.

Anxiety is just another form of entertainment. Said poet Frank O'Hara. Children are afraid of darkness. Grownups are afraid of light. Said cartoonist Robert Crumb. Our heads are round so that our thoughts can change direction. Said painter Francis Picabia. I don't know where I am anymore. Said a woman on the bus. Home is where the heart is. Said Pliny the Elder.

You might want to sit down. The language is about to start.

I've been in an odd mood ever since I discovered my autonomy. It was the magic of the Renaissance all over again. Science tries hard to keep death at bay, but time and again it turns out to be an abuse of science, and we find monstrosities wandering the forests of the world. The science we need is Otis Redding. But the science we get is a zeitgeist with a flock of insignias surrounding the president of a turd. There are no hierarchies of fruit. The apple doesn't look down on the orange. But wait till the stars come out. Wealth can mean so many things to so many people. For some it's a yacht. And for others syllables clinking on a chandelier of sound.

Most of the clutter in my brain — worries, chimeras, conjectures, rocking chairs, fantasies, beliefs — were collected in the 1960s and 1970s. The world didn't really become abrasive and mean until the 1980s, several years after Reagan got elected and Lennon got murdered. The clutter in my brain became increasingly antique and incongruous to the anathema of the coming decades. Software superseded hardware. Superstition superseded science. War superseded peace. Censorship superseded speech. And now that it's 2023 I think it's safe to say we're pretty much fucked. By "we," of course, I mean the royal we. Although there's nothing royal about us. The billionaires are doing fine. The royal we is royally fucked. And that's my pronoun.

Outside it's war. Small businesses decimated by pandemic lockdowns, inflation, the devaluing of the American dollar, supply chain crises, windows boarded up, walls graffitied, sidewalks littered with needles and feces. What appear to be extras from the Mad Max movies — helmeted, goggled, amply tattooed — whizz by on escooters and monowheels.

Inside it's Marcel Duchamp. *Nude Descending a Staircase*. Cat asleep on a blanket. Aetna healthcare letters tucked behind a paper weight, globe of glass with a big yellow flower blooming outward forever. *Cheers* on TV. 1982. That's when it all got started. The new world order. You will own nothing and be happy, Klaus Schwab tells us with an oligarchic grin.

I saw her on the way home this afternoon. One of the skinniest women I'd ever seen crawled out of a homeless tent. Of course, it's not the tent that's homeless, it's the woman. Homeless is a new adjective. It's already so slurred with meaning there's no less about it. What a strange suffix, less. It's a form of subtraction. Here's a thing you should have, but don't. Sleepless. Meatless. Seedless. Here's a thing you shouldn't have, but do. Pitiless. Purposeless. Ruthless.

The homeless encampment is growing into a village next to the vacant lot where some new office building will be erected soon full of offices no one goes to or suites and apartments only the very wealthy can afford. Too bad they can't let the homeless sleep there before the work gets underway. A few feet to the east is Westlake and yacht marinas law offices realty offices chiropractors psychotherapists houseboats kayak rentals a ketamine clinic and a cigar store.

There's even a little airport, Kenmore Air. It's amazing how those seaplanes come down on Lake Union with all those sailboats and paddle-board people and swimmers whose heads you can barely discern. I'd be freaking out if I were a pilot. I'd never land the plane. I'd fly in circles until emergency buttons bleeped. I'd land gently on a tarmac in Ephrata. And then I'd be fired.

It's nice to be greeted by blue jays when we return home from a run. They really love those peanuts. They bury them in the garden dirt and pots on the porch and then come back for more. Sadly, the squirrels in the park next door come and dig them up and replant them elsewhere.

Last year there was a homeless encampment in the park. I only got a glimpse of its occupant once. She was a gray-haired woman, sitting cross-legged in front of her tent with a book. She looked like a librarian. She vanished one day, leaving a pile of belongings behind. The city refused to clean the site up, so some neighbors banded together to expedite its removal. Luckily, they brought a Sharps Disposal box. There was a thick layer of syringes and needles that had been lying under the tent in a stratum so thick it could serve as a mattress. This isn't recreational use. This is evidence of pain, and despair. Tongs were used to pick up the needles. Tongues were used sparingly, expressly for exchanging bits of information pertinent to the situation and with a tone almost funereal in its wounded decorum. There was no casual conversation. It's dangerous to express an opinion these days. Even when there's an elephant in the room. Most definitely when there's an elephant in the room. And syringes in the grass. And bombs for Ukraine.

I've never been what you might call well-adjusted. But the world is so strange, so contrary to anything that might be conceived as rational, malaise and despair are common as crabgrass.

Edgar Allan Poe bumped into me and said his mind was on fire. There had been some kind of explosion. I looked for a cadaver that was still holding hooch. I gulped a Thunderbird. The noise calmed down a little in my head. The landscape was bleak. We were reeling from the effects of illiteracy, and the evisceration of bookstores. I invited Poe into my humble abode. That's my last Hennessy on the wall, next to Picasso's *Weeping Woman*. Hennessy is a spirit aged in oak barrels. I don't drink in real life, only in paragraphs like this, where everything is abstract, and the consequences of any statement have repercussions too distant to matter. If an empire falls because of something I said, I apologize. My bad. But the truth is, anything I write down in words disappears. The words run off with it and turn it into something a little more notable, and a little less laconic. Words like liquor, not blood. And when the dust settles, everything goes back to being what it was before, except that the entire décor has changed, and I'm drunk.

What we need is a Wang Dang Doodle. Koko Taylor gripping a microphone stand. Putting all of her energy and being and joyfulness into it. "Tonight we need no rest. / We're really gonna throw a mess. / We're gonna break out all the windows. / Gonna kick down all the doors. / We're gonna pitch a wang dang doodle /All night long." It will solve the problem. The big problem. The one with the funny tinsel and bad breath and alcoholic swagger. The one with the miniature stipulations nobody pays any attention to and the closet full of hogs and hoes and failed utopias. The big one the sweaty one the glittery one the scary one the fishnet stockinged one the one with one good eye and a polka dot bow tie and a .38 special. The one with the rigor mortis grin and a locomotive drive the one with a hand curled around a diamond studded gearshift knob. The miscarriage forgotten in the basement that day you sent your head to heaven while your feet were stuck in hell. The sticky bedroom drawer the bounced check the work in the garage the minute-to-minute miscellany of things. Each desperate delicate moment. Every lovely ivory occurrence that happened spontaneously without a serviceable rationale. The whatness of things. The sweat and hunger and sorrow of things. The kit and kaboodle and Wang Dang Doodle of things.

Mahler's "Adagietto" is sublime, one of the most beautiful things I've experienced. You might call it the B side of a Wang Dang Doodle. Dilations of light in the darkness of the circus tent that nobody sees but the eyes of the reader. But I'm groping. I know whatever words I use to describe these things will fail. And the ballerina on the back of the Percheron tumble into the sawdust.

What I'm feeling inside these words goes without saying. But I will say this: a thing is a thing as long as it's shaggy and obvious and can bump into one another like alcoholics in the San Diego Aquarium. This gives a certain suppleness to the flowers and carries you everywhere like a feeling. I will say no more about you know who, except to say that he misses you and we'll have a good laugh on Uranus. If you lean in close, you'll see that I'm up to something here. Some call it writing. Some call it obstreperous. I call it talking. I call it wet and Tuesday. Children in Spain.

I could use an elegy. A "serious reflection" on the human condition. Something suitable to my age. I choose "Not Dark Yet," by Bob Dylan. It has a real dignity to it, and a deep sadness. I listened to this song a lot when my father was dying. I bought Dylan's *Time Out of Mind* CD in which the song appears when I was making a lot of trips to the hospital. And now I'm the same age he was and this is how I got here. I kept going. I crossed a field. I crossed a street. I found a sound in my pocket. And a hole. The sound fell through the hole and slid down my leg. It felt like water. Like cold metal. Like a dime. Something slender. Something round. It's a round sound. Like the weather behind my eyes. The table I furnish with silverware. A woman I saw shaving behind a curtain of beads. The murmur of the North Pacific. And the surf in my blood.

And why do I bring all this up? I bring it up because it's pertinent to anybody with a heartbeat.

I feel light and theoretical today and amazed by airports and plums. I live in a small apartment. The rest of my life is waiting ahead. I'm not in any hurry to get there. So I sit by a rock and read a poem by André Breton and find myself in a different country. Picture a vast terrain of puddles sleeping like eyelids. You can see where this is going. The excursion is beginning to feel convex. Where does wetness come from? Hotels of ice with rooms of ice, counters of ice, elevators of ice, blankets and ice machines sitting red and redolent in the hallway, which has a floor and ceiling and chandeliers of ice. See this dial? Turn it up. It'll explain music. And the way I dress: tender buttons, road-runner pants, prehistoric shoes and a big Bermuda hat flashing on and off.

I'm wearing my running shoes to Kauai. We probably aren't going anywhere fancy. And it's a little early to pack. I wanted to wash the bath towels tonight but Molly is sleeping on them. I don't want to disturb her. She looks so comfortable. She's a very spoiled cat. This is why.

Oriana wants to get a Covid booster shot before we go to Kauai. I advise against it. I don't trust the vaccines. I did at first. Now I don't. They didn't stop transmissibility and the number of adverse effects — the ones that were reported, which I'm guessing, is the tip of the iceberg — are concerning. I once trusted science. I had enormous respect. But the science of Francis

Bacon and Robert Boyle and Isaac Newton is long gone. Scientific research is now funded by corporations, and corporations get the results most favorable to the corporation. Big Pharma especially.

I'm grateful for my underwear. It feels like the soft muzzle of a horse, nudging me forward. Now I know what is meant by magic underwear. At job interviews, I would describe myself as pervasive, not unlike a gas. I don't give a shit about the modern world. It's all hard right angles and flaccid, totalitarian screeds. We've all been there: that dreaded phone call to the healthcare organization. We should all be receiving stipends from God. When the sun rises tomorrow, will there still be a world? Subjectivity is just a homunculus on a Ferris wheel. There are medicines available for this. Ask Philippus Aureolus Theophrastus Bombastus von Hohenheim, a.k.a. Paracelsus. Remember him? Wish he was still around. Anybody other than Dr. Fugazi.

I feel Molly's claws in my leg. She does this frequently when I'm sitting at my desk. It means she wants to be fed. Some of the time she just wants attention. Her favorite food is fish. Tuna, salmon, trout. I don't get it. I can't stand fish. It has a foul odor. It reminds me of the smell of trash dumpsters in back of restaurants. The preferred habitat of rats, despair, despondency, Schopenhauerian rotgut symposiums, glop, goo, gelatinous camaraderie, cruise ship tampons fished out of the Sound, bloody surgical gowns, skeletal remains and other unspeakably weird shit you can come across anywhere. But Molly loves it. Inhales it. I stand by, holding my nose.

I wash some bath towels. I like washing bath towels. They smell so good and they're so easy to fold. And the first time they're used they feel so good against the skin. Soft, absorbent, almost matrimonial. The towel slides from the rack softly. I smell its perfume on my face. I could dance with it. After I pull the towels out of the washer I spin the drum around to make sure there's nothing stuck to it. Sometimes I'll hear the clankety-clank of a nickel or quarter, sometimes a paper clip, and fish it out. We share the laundry with other tenants. Sometimes I'll see a quarter or nickel lying on top of the washer. Maybe they're intended for the laundry fairy. Who's the laundry fairy? I'm the laundry fairy.

I saw a woman recently wearing a T-shirt that said "YOUR ANXIETY IS LYING TO YOU." That cracks me up. I wish that were true. My anxieties tell me awful things. And I'm terrible at denial. I try my hardest to deny the reality of certain things and if that doesn't work, I follow Rumi's advice and treat each fear and despair as a house guest. I offer everything I can to appease the spirit: wine, coffee, tea, cannabis gummies. Gummies are the best. Anxiety scoffs at coffee.

Here's one I can't get out of my head. There's a lot of things I can't get out of my head. But this one thing is really sticky. Exceptionally stubborn. It's something I read a couple of days ago, an excerpt from *The Cherry Battle*, by Günther Anders, which is a dialogue with Hannah Arendt, to whom he'd been married for a few years. He asks her if they didn't have the mindset of employees, even though both were independent writers. He wondered if what they believed to be original ideas had in fact been dictated, so that whatever work, even work that seemed totally spontaneous, independent, and the most original was probably a *"travail de commande,"* work made to order. Work influenced, however subtly, by a sponsor. Writing, in other words, geared to reap a reward, though not necessarily monetary. A reward in form of social prestige, acceptance into a group or coveted academic community. Even the idea of independence itself had been inculcated. But the illusion of independence must be stringently maintained. Servants who don't consider themselves free are suspected of disloyalty. "Is that what we've become," Arendt asks Anders with vehemence. Anders shrugged his shoulders. "Maybe."

The wizard fingers never rest. Wrote Emily Dickinson. What were her fingers like? Thin and elegant, or surprisingly thick and strong? Soft and pale, or leathery and sunburn? Or a combination of all of these, depending on the season? I'll bet she had dirt under her fingernails. Judging by the number of insects and flowers in her work, she appears to have spent a lot of time in the garden. Wizard makes sense to me: those are gnarled, arthritic fingers, twisted by learning.

Stuck indoors today. Couldn't run. More wildfire smoke. A shame. Such a gorgeous day otherwise. October 2nd and it's like summer, 73°. There are wildfires going all over the state. This has been the driest year on record. The closest one is the Bolt Creek fire, up by Skykomish. It's been burning for almost a month now and has destroyed 12,142 acres. For which a crew of 152 personnel has been allocated, two engines, one dozer, two water tenders, and 79 overhead. This is a joke. They need ten times this number to contain the fire. Multiple airtankers. Dozens of dozers. Hundreds of personnel for every 1,000 acres. I can't imagine the exhaustion and frustration of the personnel who continue to fight this fire in rugged terrain.

This planet is getting fried. I envy the religious. I'd have faith that God would eventually intervene. What a luxury that would be. I wish I could take my incredulity out back and shoot it.

Why not look to supernatural intervention? Nobody really knows the fundamental reality of the universe, all being, all existence, every unreasonable weed and daisy, the kit and kaboodle.

In 1928, Paul Dirac postulated the existence of positively charged electrons. The result was an equation — the Dirac equation, a relativistic wave equation explaining that parity inversion (sign inversion of spatial coordinates) is symmetrical for all half-spin electrons and quarks — that described a free particle in motion which has not only positive energy solutions, but negative ones as well. Don't worry, I don't understand any of this either. But here's what's amazing: it was the equation that led Dirac to this knowledge, not Dirac. He was as surprised as anyone else. This is astonishing. If equations can point to hidden realities and unsuspected dimensions, I'd like to get my hands on some chalk and a blackboard and start scribbling some equations. Trouble is, I suck at math, much less equations. I'm stuck doing haiku, and distilling metaphors, the kind that sublimate in a bowl of bouillabaisse, or precipitate syllables into silicates of prose.

Here's another of Dirac's obsessions: Cher. Dirac loved Cher. He bought his own color TV just so he would watch her. Not surprising. She's a fascinating equation. A volatile cocktail of charisma and talent with a smile the size of Miami.

There's a lot of things I don't have words for. The sound a bottle of carbonated beverage makes when I turn the cap slightly to let some pressurized air out. There's no word for that. I need a Dirac to come up with a word for that. Or an equation or set of equations to reveal phenomena I've never even dreamed of. If you managed to get Dirac and Dickinson together — *i.e.,* poetry and physics, you'd have a human equation of limitless possibility. And if you put a Bukowski and a Rilke together, you'd have a monster explosion of roses and beer. An Artaud a Rimbaud and a Poe would bond to create a carnal dimension of blue velvet in a Texas roadhouse. Sand on the dance floor. Neon horse in a mad gallop. Light and diaphana. Anthropopathism and absinthe.

A woman with a voice like silk on a summer day. That breeze blowing the curtain into the room in *Bright Star*, Fanny Brawne lying on a bed in a light dress that balloons with the same breeze as she reads a letter from Mr. John Keats. It is at this point that we must put our fingers on true value. I hold in my hands a glimmer of understanding. Its wings are transparent and blue and prepared to fly. I can see heaven through them, and Ted Berrigan sitting in a chair. I know a cat named Way-Out Willie, had a cool little chick named Rockin' Billie, made a heart of stone Susie-Q doin that crazy hand jive too. Baby on YouTube I saw yesterday, looking around, minutes old, seeing the world for the first time. That's it. That's what you want art to do.

Writing is herds of words in a Texas wind storm. It's all about shouts and lightning and Texans singing about hell. Principles have their place, but rants will get you further down the road. It helps to ponder the vagaries of mammograms. Learn how to look inside people. Imagine a man going down into the world of the dead and finding snow drifting down slowly in still air, the ground littered with junk bonds and credit default swaps. Or the state of pornography in 1971. Bulbous taboos for pulpous tattoos. The soap in Flaubert's kitchen. Floorboards creaking in a Deadwood hotel. Charles Baudelaire sitting down to breakfast. A man splitting a geode in half with a vice, water gushing out from a rainy day in the Cretaceous period, all predicates and sand.

What if you went through life trying to keep yourself a secret. How would that be done? You could try being someone else, or speak and write in the most unaffected manner possible, so neutral that you'd be like a mass of frigid air, or lichen on a rock, or rungs on a ladder. Going up? Going down? I don't care. I'm just here to help you achieve your goals. I have no opinion good or bad about anything. No passions. No desires. I think I'm ready. Ready now to enter the workforce. Which has become a minefield. The colleges being the most dangerous of all.

At the behest of a friend, Oriana and I watch a Netflix documentary about infinity. Various mathematicians and physicists give their versions. An analogy is given: an infinity hotel. A hotel with an infinite number of rooms. Which would entail an infinite staff. Infinite sheets and towels. An elevator able to travel at the speed of light just to get you to your room in a timely fashion. We collapse under the weight of the analogy. The physicists struggle with their outlook on infinity. I try to keep up with the math. Can't do it. Infinity makes me sleepy. My eyes close without my even being aware of it and when they open a woman is saying that to be conscious is to be wrangling with infinity. Sounds a bit like Jacob wrestling with God. How did that turn out? I like Eugène Delacroix's version best: Jacob goes at God with all his might as God (in the form of an angel) appears sternly in control of the whole thing. It's an exhausting match. It goes all night. Jacob, still undefeated, is crippled. Nobody wins or loses. He ceases struggling. I'm presuming that that's also how to deal with infinity. Cease struggling. Leave infinity alone.

Here's what I found in infinity: nothing. My brain and infinity don't get along. My brain doesn't understand infinity and infinity can't find anywhere comfortable to lie down in my brain.

And I just had it reupholstered. If I could think in the terms of calculus, I could go much further. But I have the same problems with calculus that I have with infinity. What I need is some ether. Either some ether or some algebra either will do. But if I were me, I would go for the ether. And crawl into some algebra when I feel the time is right. Let X represent my need for the fourth dimension. Then multiply each variable with a song and a Belgian waffle. Almost any scenario can be generated from arbitrary sets. If an octave contains grapes, then the sound of the wind must be unfurling in a vineyard. Here the answer depends on ivy. Take vector X as an example, in which case X is a turntable and Y is a cloud. The difference between patronage and upbringing is ragweed plus unicorn divided by whimsy. Multiplied by the square root of quibble, the product will be gigantic, shiny, and sympathetic to the vibrations of yucca near Beaumont, Texas.

1963. Don't know why that year fascinates me so much. Was it the year I first heard The Beatles? I believe so, though I hadn't been that taken by them initially. I was into R&B and Motown, Mary Wells, Doris Troy, the Shirelles, The Crystals, Martha Reeves and the Vandellas. "Louis Louis" by the Kingsmen, a primal, garage-band song that relishes its crudeness with jubilant insouciance, marked a step away from pop song innocence into adolescent decadence. That was memorable. 1963 was the first time I got drunk, which was a revelation. I had no idea one could alter one's mood and outlook so easily. The lyrics are hilariously simple. "Louis, Louis, / oh, no, me gotta go. / Louis, Louis, / oh baby, me gotta go." It's all about a girl: "A fine little girl, she waits for me / Me catch the ship aross the sea / Me sailed that ship all alone / Me never think I'll make it home." I presume they were shooting for a Jamaican vibe. But that's not what comes across. The song is too raunchy.

The lyrics — which I doubt anyone really paid attention to — is too raw for the tenderness of romance. It sounds like a dazed young man on a three-day binge in Barbados.

I go for a run. September is an odd month. It's like the last day of a carnival in which some of the stands have begun packing up, so if you're going to have some fun, you'd better get on it.

There's a small, wooded section along the pedestrian walkway by Westlake between a couple of boat marinas where the city just yesterday deposited some rich black dirt. The dirt looks so rich and enticing I want to stand in it and bury my feet and take root so that by a combination of fairy tale magic and will I can turn myself into a pumpkin. I see myself a few days later adorning someone's porch, my brain replaced by a candle, my face carved into an eerily cheerful grin glowing goldenly in the October night. Happy to have experienced dirt. Rich black dirt. So fertile it could turn a toothpick into a sequoia or a seventy-five-year-old man into a pumpkin with an insane grin.

I return home and take a shower and Oriana returns from her plant shopping expedition with a fern and a hellebore. The hellebore will go in the spot previously occupied by the hydrangea. The fern will go in front of our living room window. I marvel at Oriana's newfound passion for plants. And how sad it is to see everything so parched by drought. Summer 2022 is officially the driest summer on record in Seattle.

Here I am contemplating life. I do that from time to time. How can you not? Especially toward the end. It was a lot more fun when I drank. Thinking takes on a certain swagger, a devil-may-care, swashbuckling panache. Wagnerian music harnessed to the breath. It's time for caressing old wounds. Redeeming old feelings for new perceptions. Viewed soberly, lucidly, life looks a little more like an old coat in the closet. A bit frayed around the cuffs. A mysterious stain on the left sleeve. An old copy of Apollinaire in the right pocket. Crumpled bit of paper once wrapped a straw. The inevitable lint. A little pain hops by in the form of a frog. Pain is always a little amphibious. It starts out with a little carpentry then morphs into an ambience amenable to deep reflection: alligators, cypress, duckweed, and spider lilies. And then a big groove forms in your soul with a needle reading its modulations and shooting Etta James out of a nearby speaker. This is a morphology I now recognize as the funny winter effulgence of a long welcome rest. At last.

When direction exceeds the current, you must glue a goldfish to the periphery of your diction. Diction is the direction your voice will take when it becomes a handstand. I'm going on an excursion in an armchair it's an armchair excursion yesserreebob. I've got a green light baby I'm moving on. Sinking swarms with levers you should pull one and see what happens. A conflagration of magnets convinced me attraction is all about fanfare. Robert Plant singing a Townes Van Zandt song in Red Rocks, Colorado. About nothingness. Oblivion. A voice echoing off the obsidian hardness of a Colorado night. When I reach the bottom I'll give you a shout. That's your cue to stop reading this sentence and fly a fever kite over a pile of frozen windows. Any excuse at all for misbehaving is what you call a poem. Break the windows. Bust down the door. Get a basket fill it with trinkets ingots buckles and gold. Bring it to me. I'll hand you a poem. Filled to the brim with lampshades pentameter meadowlarks and hellebore.

Ted Berrigan once sold a pint of blood to buy some typing paper. That impresses me. That level of dedication must come from some inner sustenance. I'm not sure how to frame it. As a young man I would get it immediately. There would be nothing perverse about it. I would not call him a martyr to the muse. But as an old man I'm more vulnerable to the vagaries of the world. Life is brief. You can take that to the bank. But first look inside. When a feeling is oceanic and unsectarian you should go to a blood bank. Otherwise, I'd just stay home with a little laudanum, "half in love with easeful death." Nothingness isn't like garlic. It's more like a horse. Words are a different story. It's why people sit in their parked cars gazing at the lights of Los Angeles. Everything in the universe flirts with the glitter of absence. And for that, words are ideal.

I like to dangle. I'll take a stand on a question and dangle from that. By definition, I'm not natural. It's a question of being open and direct rather than mettlesome and phagocytotic. I'm not a microbe. I'm a virus. I'm a contagion of priors committed in youth. I'm medicated these days and calm as a close friend holding a big fish. If you can guess what kind of fish, you're a huckleberry. Water is an important partner of our daily maternity. This is why I wear a derby in honor of deep guttural sounds. I wear the icing of piracy in recognition of all that is done in stealth and superfluity. I wear the ring of bravado and crave the attention of traffic cops. I wear the stubble of learning in a hurry to catch a syllabus. I'm not entirely here. I won't say what I am. Or where I am. I won't to commit to anything too final or orchestrated. I like to dangle.

I'm lying on the bed watching *Le Journal de France 2* on my laptop. Oriana comes in and asks if I'd heard anything more about the sewer work today. A man came out to check the condition of the pipe this afternoon. He ran a video camera snake down the pipe. The moving image appeared on a nearby computer screen.

I told her no, not yet. Are you familiar with Annie Ernaux? No, I'm not. Who is she? An author. She won the Nobel Prize today for her life in literature.

I still think about the weirdness of Bob Dylan getting the Nobel Prize for literature. It's weird because I grew up with his music and words, primarily the period between *Another Bob Dylan* and *Blonde on Blonde*, which was a thrill to the nerves and a circus for the mind. His language was fantastic. These weren't songs, these Molotov cocktails of Dadaesque wit and verve, aimed at all the Western institutions and doctrines and habits and established ways of doing things and thinking. So for this guy to age into a figure of such global renown and respect is rather astonishing. And yes, I believe he deserved the award. Absolutely. Even though it was a blow to the book industry. It didn't do much to promote reading. My favorite Dylan album isn't a record it's a book. The book is *Tarantula*, and I like to let it crawl around in my mind.

Dinner tonight was good. All our dinners are good. Oriana does all the cooking. She was a chef in an upper scale restaurant when I met her twenty-nine years ago. We had pulled pork and apple pie and watched episode 2 of *The Lincoln Lawyer* on Netflix. I did the dishes. Oriana cooks. I do dishes. It's a nice balance.

I'm ok with dishes. I don't mind doing dishes. Maybe a little. It's a bit tedious. But largely I like the feel of things, the forms of things, slippery with soap, so they must be handled with care, attention, so you notice things, the circumstances promote a nice level of awareness. I'd rather rinse a glass than get a subpoena. I remember, age fifteen, my job as a dishwasher in a Chinese restaurant, shaking the wok, I filled it with soap and water and dumped all the cutlery into it and shook it and shook it and shook it. I ate all the uneaten sweet and sour pork. I like the feeling of the sponge. I like to squeeze it. Squeezing things is naturally pleasurable. Warm water too. Warm water always feels good. That said, I wouldn't want to wash dishes for eight hours. Anything done repetitively for eight or nine hours is going to suck. But think about it. Ponder the interactions we have with handles and knobs and wheels and ladders. With tools. Tool-beings are good in Heidegger's eyes, since they hint at a layer of reality deeper than all access. The long beak of the ibis is good for rooting out crustaceans in estuarial mud and such. If there is a quiddity of shape the glass, the plate, the frying pan and long beak of the ibis are supremely charmed. Thought bubbles up and pops. Thought doesn't have a shape. Thought is more like water, flowing around shapes, lifting concepts, calculating time, invent-ing reasons to do things, or not do things, or turning to vapor and vanishing. Heat is energy transfer. Thought is the energy it takes to enter a kitchen with a firm resolve to do the dishes. Did Buckminster Fuller do dishes? Yes, I'm certain he did. This is the man who said ninety-nine percent of who you are is invisible and untouchable. The sink is a sudsy suburb of the lost isle of Atlantis. There are bubbles, sponges, and the cacophony of cut-lery in a hodgepodge of soapy ablution. Wheatgrass in a shot glass. A broiled bonito on bone china. Germs destroyed by liq-uid Dawn. Matter probed in a synchrotron.

I had my beginning in late summer in Minneapolis, Minnesota. Minneapolis has this in common with Paris: a river runs through the city. Trees and buildings are reflected on its surface. I had a nice ongoing relationship with that river. I liked its turtles and carp and catfish and mud.

But is that where I'm from? What is it to be from something? I'm from a seed. A zygote. A pairing of energies. A war. A junk-yard romance. A road to nowhere. The roaming of Rome. I don't know where I'm from. I just arrived. Squirming wiggling flailing appealing for sustenance and understanding, like everyone else. This is why voices do so well to blend in harmony. This was the source of a lot of reflection and reading and speculating and dream. And then I got old.

Wherever I was from, I would've liked, in order to die, to have a music that was more my own, more alive in sympathy and oddities of generally misguided emotion, like irony, or seclusion. Is there a way to make music with what you've got inside your olive? Your ever so lovely olive. It's alive. Your olive. Alive and olive. Are there sounds? Sounds for this? Sounds for the olive alive in alien jars of jukebox overture? You can howl. You can roar. You can whisper. You can spit. You can bend a note into a beautiful woman. You can squeak. Pushing music with a drum can be done, it's all that precedes the turbulence of poetry, all the cold cuts, the ecstasies, the muted trumpet that heralds the epiphanies of the closet. Cans of tomato. Boxes of pasta. A jar of olives. Air Force jacket. Jackson Pollock pants. Patti Smith's T-shirt. Bob Dylan's sunglasses.

Stuck inside again today. Couldn't run. The wildfire smoke covered the city. Air quality was in the "unhealthy for certain groups range." Frustrated by the immovable high pressure system keeping all this smoke locked in and any hope for rain a thin and distant fantasy of self-deception, I looked at the NASA satellite map and saw threadlike wisps of smoke blown into ubiquitous haze over the entire Pacific northwest, save for the few towns along the coast.

I distract myself with *Hamlet*, French verbs, and the dried roots of secular variables. The world is so easily abused. It could use some enchantment. Technocracy is so sterile. Milk from a mechanical cow. Thoughts of escape drift through our conversation like secret stashes of money.

The winds today are a theater of thread. What was sewn minutes ago is forgotten by the time we get to the door and leave. Everything unravels, even the equations for magic twine. I could see a foundry showing off. A man stood outside juggling planets as a dream of locomotion moved forward under a shower of sparks. The world got prettier. It became a full-strength paradise. I felt suddenly available. A little ruffled. Even a little rational. The circumstances were perfect for making butter. I could sense it in the vocabulary lying around. Quantum tints of meringue shook like a tiger in the word *sparrow*. None of this is true, of course, it's all just a matter of geometry, the frolic of cubes and parallels. Things are felt, things are considered, things become words. Almost any carpenter can tell you how to handle lumber. What they won't tell you is how to crochet a sock with a sunny predicate and a quantum jackhammer. It's easy. Find an almanac. Then spend an hour substantiating all of its claims. This will cause a mustache to appear on your chin, wiry and round like a framework of time. You now have full authority to help a sad perplexity find its way to a defense lawyer. This will make a good TV show. I promise. But when the police get here, I'd appreciate it if you didn't mention anything about poetry.

Here come the organisms. All creatures great and small. Led by Captain Beefheart. You can't keep a man like that down for long. The Beefheart organism is choc-a-bloc with organelles. Donkeys with doubts and doings and dongs. Guinea pigs pirouetting on the backs of elephants. Ichthyologists swimming libidinal waters. Shy quiet pools of turquoise ringed by Sonoran desert toads. Zebras in skirts. Giraffes in drafts. Crows in ice cream bowls. Mosquitos with proboscises as big as phonograph needles. The Animals. The Monkees. The Eagles. Iron Butterfly. The Stray Cats. Blue Oyster Cult. The Byrds. T Rex. Government Mule. Grizzly Bear. Atomic Rooster.

Those times when nothingness clings to your nerves and works the soil into permeable grits.

Here is what I can do for you: nothing. I can't do a thing for you until you tell me what it is you want me to do. I can be a boxing partner or float you into the trees with my ambient charm.

I want to be like a wilderness of snow and provoke the jingling of reindeer.

I want to be rocks. I want to be sleep. I want to be a tree that rocks in the wind like sleep.

You want language to attain music. It attains the sense of music not in sound but in its attitude. Attitude in aviation means orientation to the horizontal plane. It is much the same in music, as when the rhythm mimics the landscape of the human heart, and all the buffalo scatter as the train moves down the rails, the ties still reeking of creosote, I'm guessing that odor may have been in Neal Cassady's nose before he collapsed from exhaustion and died. There is music for this and the music is inconsolably sad. But underlying all music is a sense of defiance. Music is not of this Earth and it knows it and flaunts it, flaunts it beautifully in the angelic voices of women and the source of all voices which is breath, which is air, which is so thin and delicate you can't see it, but it's strong enough to support a cargo plane weighing over a ton, and that's just the wind.

If it's Lizst, it spits, if it's Bach, it's back to back, and if it's Mozart, it's more than art, it's linen.

Down here in the dirt nothing hurts. The music of dirt is a music of worms. Roots and mushrooms. Correspondences. It's a big all-encompassing melody sewn with the stars in the still of night, Juliet in the mausoleum, on her knees with a knife. This is the music of yearning. Tim Buckley's "Song to the Sirens." Sung by Elizabeth Fraser. The call of seals on the shores of Moray Firth. Music isn't mere sounds. It's a zone, a place where nothing hurts.

Chewing is fun. Almost anything to do with the mouth is fun. Especially talking. Talking to someone with whom you feel comfortable talking. Talking requires that qualifier. Talking to strangers, especially in the U.S., can be a chore. People don't open up readily. They do in California. You can talk to almost anyone in California with the kind of ease and daring that the language appreciates, it's everything a language lives for, the spontaneity of speech. Among friends. Among strangers. In bus depots. Airports. Conversations in airports are always a little subdued. It's the high security. All the humiliating things they — the powers that be — force you to do for security. It's not working. These measures don't augment my sense of security they erode it. They give me the heebie-jeebies. Bus depots and train stations are much more conducive. Music explodes it. You get people around music and they're either going to dance or talk a lot. Shout things. Most people trying to keep the mood buoyant and avoid touchy subjects. I don't. I can't. I've got an allergy to small talk, but even in social groups where I should know better, I end up saying something that provokes, inflames, disturbs, causes people to walk away. This is why I like writing. There's nobody there to offend. You're not going to disturb anyone. But if you do (and yes, it's a distinct possibility these days), they can just put the book down and go elsewhere. This is a disappointment to language which wants everyone to join in no matter what and bring as much opposition and nuance and difference of opinion to the mix as possible. Homogeneity kills. But what can you do? Gavage is unethical. You shouldn't force feed people one's opinions. But hey. You can climb into a sentence anytime and go on a journey. If you use the same kind of attention as going down a wild river in an inflatable raft, you'll be amazed at what a few words can do. Right now there's a lot of drought. Think of this as rain. A rain dance.

I held a bag of nails. They were shaking with thunder. I also had a hammer, a propeller, and a rattlesnake. I was about to describe reality from a subatomic point of view. I sat next to a tidepool on the coffee table and played bingo with an engorged sense of abandon. I ignited the clocks with my feather boas and my sometime flair for fun. Perceptual distortions get me off. Symmetry makes me nervous. It's so militaristic. And uniform. I like the funk of testimony. The fragrance of surgery. The dribble of gargoyles. The tinsel of floats. Tonight I witnessed something in the garden moving. Was it the roses, or the presence of an invisible spirit, Ereshkigal or Elvis Presley? I did see a body of words glitter. I wrote them down, but as I wrote them down, they stopped glittering. They turned into shouts. Have faith, I shouted back, once you're in motion maturity and wisdom will follow. You will resume your glitter. Catch fire and bite things. Shatter the mirrors crack the beams. And burn a big hole in the logic of everything.

I'm drowning in propaganda these days. I don't know what to believe. I am trapped in a subjective contusion. Everything is black and blue. If there's one thing I can trust, it's pain. Pain never lies. But who wants pain? That's not a good way to get the news. You'll find yourself in a languor of unshaven stubble wondering what to do about the drip in the sink, the smoke in the air, world leaders threatening nuclear war, future hospitable bills, the inevitable decay of the body, inflation, people working too many jobs to read, the growth of illiteracy, the spread of censorship, the hummingbirds in the park where a limb broke off a laurel due to the drought, the canary in the cave that is Jackson, Mississippi, government turning its back on its citizens, the preposterous hoax that is the subjunctive mood, and what a tizzy it's put me in, wishing when I should be fishing, washing clothes, building alliances, adding the final touches to my spaceship.

There are minerals of the heart that extrude in a greasy luster and explode on contact with banality. We call these chrysocolla stalactites. At night, when the icy winds come blowing in from Lake Michigan, they glow like radiators in a Chicago brothel. This is in no way intended to substitute for hindsight, or bourbon. I want these words to be real words and do what words do without the encumbrance of mimicry, or cabinet making. This is not a restricted zone. I'm open to anything, including papaya, stanchions, and airplanes. I'm not against technology. I'm not entirely in love with it, either. But if you're waiting to take off, taxi to the end of this sentence and wait for a sign from God. The weather today is deeply uncertain. You can tell by the way the sky sits down on the mountains and reclines there creating snow and skunk cabbage. The ponds represent the sediment of clarity. Telescopes into the microbial realm. The indentations left by the legs of a dubitative mood. When *Hello, Dolly!* opened in Detroit in November, 1963, I was fifteen and had just bought a motorcycle with the money I made as a dishwasher in a Chinese restaurant. It's hard to put this within the context of a forest, and for that reason it has been left out. Instead, I'm bringing in a chorus of dignified matrons to sing "Insane Asylum," by Willie Dixon, backed by an orchestra of gargoyles and elves. Each violin will be varnished with the blood of a dragon and cured in the sunshine of the Cretaceous period, ferns dripping with the honey of eternity.

Suspicion, like a finger, touches my forehead now and then, and I ponder things askance, critically, but not too critically, just enough to expand my attention and bring me into a closer relationship with things. Once I get past the patterns, I begin to see the imperfections, and it's the imperfections that season admiration with a madcap

I lose all objectivity around loss. I don't do well with loss. There are some things you can't pull away from, distance oneself to achieve a comfortably transcendent view. Objectivity is a chimera. Perception is colored by cognitive bias. Not to mention the need for illusion, for a narrative framework that gives meaning and a moral import to the vagaries of chaos. Experience is immune to belief. Loss is quite real. Every time I lose someone close to me a dull rusty nail is pounded into my heart. That's not an objective occurrence. Everything is entangled, interrelated, mingled, blended, fused. Human consciousness is a bouillabaisse of strange crustaceans and the simmer of Mediterranean water. The glow of bioluminescent phytoplankton off Puerto Marqués beach in Acapulco, or the gentle lapping of neural oscillations on the shores of cognition.

The objective viewpoint assumes that there is an external, one-dimensional, objective reality. This is wrong. The universe is a Wang Dang Doodle of epic incongruities and contradictions. The dilemma of wave-particle duality, for example, or the fact quarks have no size, are 2% mass and 98% potential and kinetic energy, or that electrons have the ability to be in two separate places simultaneously, pulls the rug out from any attempt to view the universe logically.

The air was good today. We finally got some inshore winds to get rid of the wildfire smoke. Hopefully, it didn't blow with enough intensity to create a problem several hundred miles to the east, where the fires are occurring. It was nice to be able to open a few windows a crack and get rid of some of the moisture that's been building up. Oriana noticed the carpet felt humid, as it did the few days after we had it cleaned last spring. The flap on my desk still sticks a little. We went for a run down by Lake Union. Not a single cloud in the sky. Freakish for Seattle. I peaked into a corner coffeehouse on the way back in the hopes they might have some jelly doughnuts or Bismarks. It's in a glass and steel building that went up a couple of years ago, replacing a 7-Eleven and a funky old apartment building. They had nothing. Just some muffins by the cash register. It never ceases to amaze me how joyless and sterile these newer coffeehouses and small cafés are, reflecting what has been a radical shift toward a digitalized world. The words *coffeehouse* and *café* are misnomers. These places are far too sterile to deserve that kind of nomenclature. A few have begun refusing cash. Don't see how that's legal. But it is. Though it may not be in the future. The Payment Choice Act was reintroduced to the House of Representatives in July 2021, the goal of which is to preserve cash as an essential payment choice. The techno-tyrant plutocrats want everyone to use electronic and contactless methods of payment, which would inevitably lead to a social credit system. I hope the bill passes. I like cash. It's so easy. Private and tangible. A simple transaction without extraneous technology. No surveillance. No tracking device. We're not animals. We don't need to be hunted. Especially at this vulnerable moment, buying a cruller.

6:55 P.M. October. I heard a bird outside the bedroom window. A robin. Always so cheerful sounding, those birds. Such a joy to hear at 5:00 on a spring morning. Long time since I was able to get up that early. Wonder how their lungs are after all that wildfire smoke. Hummingbirds especially. Haven't seen any in the park for a while. Where do they go? Beginning to get dark early now. People recede into their secret lairs like cephalopods. Food assumes more relish. Rumination grows into illumination. Bright lights of Christmas. All those songs. How weird we have world leaders clamoring for nuclear war. Utterly callous. The stern look of misery on the faces of pentagon generals. Murderous. Bloodthirsty. Hungry for power. Jackets plastered with medals. They're like talismans. What deep insecurities they must disguise. Hence the obsession with arms. Deep down they must know what they're doing is fucked up. But they do it anyway.

A mourner walking among the children, smiling. The idea was to hide the tragedy inside. The nails of mortality clawing at the heart. Urgency pounding against the ribcage. Kids don't need to know about this shit. Though some get an early peek. Grandma or grandpa in an open casket. The morticians did a good job. They look like they're resting. But there's an indefinable stillness that's quite unmistakable. And that's death. Imagine the thickest steel door your mind is capable of creating. Try pounding on it. Your fists will hurt. And no, the door won't open. Ever. Not for eternity. And that's death. Though I did like the way Rod Serling presented it in Episode 81, "Nothing in the Dark," in which death — in the guise of Robert Redford — the dashing Sundance Kid, but playing a kindly cop here — visits Wanda Dunn in her squalid about-to-be-demolished apartment building, who has allowed him because he was wounded and begging for help, and when his reality becomes apparent, Wanda surrenders to his gentility and allows him to escort her into the afterlife. I hear John Trudell's words were, "My ride's here." That sounds about right.

If I walk around bemoaning a dominion, this would be the dominion of drums and lovely faces. Feather boas and naked women. Tech billionaires and burning men. This is a nutty dominion. A dominion of nuts. And squeezing and falling and people taking their time. The dominion before this dominion, the dystopic proliferation of weaponry and endless war, militarized police and crappy doughnuts, even the Oscars has begun looking deteriorated and weird. The red carpet looks frayed and the movie stars look nervous and afraid. That other dominion was far from perfect. It wasn't Eden it wasn't Camelot it wasn't Cockaigne, but it had 7-Elevens where you could get beer and cigarettes if it was Thanksgiving and you were from out of town and forgot it was Thanksgiving. Cheap motels with decent TVs. Midnight sagas of mints and hammers and LSD. Garage bands. Diabolic pumpkins. Charming lawn sprinklers. And lots of good clean water. Leg room and free meals on passenger jets. Swarms of boardwalk darlings. Genuine smiles. The night falling from the sky over Boise. The smell of sage. Wind through an open window.

I'm still searching for a delinquent palace. A place where I can allow the architecture to blossom in whatever manner it chooses. I think of architecture as a living force. Take floats and airplane propellers, for example. You can see the DNA right at the surface. The marriage of function and beauty. Logic crashing in a beautiful dome of ice and fire. Physical laws challenged with eloquent aplomb. The plumbing of angels the wiring of wizards. These are my digs. My unmanageable halls. Eloquent delinquent and huge. Humped like a whale. Chromatic as a glass.

Several weeks back Oriana signed us up for flu shots at the local grocery, Syphway. The old one, the one we went to for years on upper Queen Anne, is gone. In its place is a huge hole. A property development company is constructing a seven-story building of luxury apartments which will house the new Syphway beneath. We went to the one on lower Queen Anne, a.k.a. Uptown. We both hate driving down there. It's overcrowded, the streets are confusing after having been reconfigured with bicycles lanes and bus lanes, efforts to manage the homeless problem have been spasmodic and mostly cosmetic, the sidewalks are littered with trash, urine, and human fecal matter. I went to make a right turn for the Syphway underground parking garage but had to wait for a crazy man to finish his crazy dance in the crosswalk. I parked in the garage and we took the elevator up. We passed a group of customers slavishly checking and bagging their groceries. You'd think they'd get a discount for doing this work. But no, they do not. Nobody protests. Nobody says a thing. There are no grunts, no sneers, no malcontents. It is what Leni Riefenstahl told John Pilger she called the unsettling indifference of the German people during the Third Reich, a "submissive void." A more obvious example of this is the permissive silence of the public regarding the war in Ukraine. Hardly a soul is protesting the bellicose language of our president and his administration for continuing to prod Russia into a nuclear war. The public seems catatonic. I don't know what it is. Hypnosis? Brainwashing?

Oriana got both her flu shot and Covid booster shot, but the pharmacy was out of the higher dosage of flu vaccine for people over sixty-five. How can this be? I had an appointed time for my shots. I received two reminder messages. How is it possible they didn't think to put aside a dosage for someone who'd made an appointment? Imagine making a reservation at an upscale restaurant and arriving to find that they'd given your table to someone else and there would be no available tables for several hours. Are pharmacists still capable of doing math?

Chalk it up to the dark side of the Wang Dang Doodle. The chaos of a public in drunken indignation. But without a language to dignify the indignation. So the indignant fume in silence while the imbecilic lead the way. But this is not a true Wang Dang Doodle. There are many aspects to the Wang Dang Doodle. Many cuts, many faces, many planes, many distortions. It's prismatic. And blastematic. Because the Wang Dang Doodle has a good side. A very good side.

I'm an inebriate of air. Thanks to some inshore winds, we had some good air today. Sweet, clear, oxygen-rich air. I was able to go for another long run by Lake Union before another shroud of smoke blew west from the fires in the Cascades. There were a lot of strong runners out. That was good to see. The exquisite Aquavit of exertion. "Inebriate of Air" is not a phrase I coined. It's from an Emily Dickinson poem. "Inebriate of air — am I — / And Debauchee of Dew — / Reeling — thro' endless summer days — / From inns of molten Blue —." So there. Take that Shitty Fucked Up Century Of Idiot Tycoons, homicidal warmongers, and globalized rape of the planet. I'm an inebriate of air. At least when the air isn't lousy with smoke. When the air clears, I shall but drink the more!

What do you think of me? Never mind. I don't know what I think of me. I know I shall be brief, as all men. And women, whose lives and loves are so different that it makes me more than a little delighted to be this confused this late in life. I'll never know the feeling of having breasts or a vagina, but I did come to know the general impulses and needs of the body, the human body, what did Shakespeare call it, a poor, bare, forked animal. The image is ungainly. Life is ungainly. Humans lack the grace of swans and cats. We're primates, don't pretend otherwise, and lug ourselves around like rocking boats. Like drunken lords. Like a monkey on a bicycle. So this is a part of me. It's not unique. I'm unique, yes, there's uniqueness in everyone. It's not a reliable quality. Not if you're looking for identity. Or try to discover the identity that's been you all along rocking the boat and putting heavy feet on the ground after a night of dreams and rubbing the eyes and rising to wrestle the fugitive day. Identity doesn't matter nearly as much as crackling with ecstasy in a sci-fi drama involving werewolves, Romania, and beautiful women. All you'll ever need in life is a good hat, a warm coat, some antibiotics, and a little equipoise.

I hear a pounding drum, a butterfly appears and lands on a red doorhandle. It's the ad currently running before the French news and anchor lady Anne-Sophie Lapix (a news anchor is called a *présentatrice* in French) appears. Today she is wearing a white lowcut blouse under a black jacket with thin, threadlike white stripes, black pants and black shoes. The top story is *la pénurie de carburant*, the gas shortage, due to an oil refinery strike. The lines at the gas stations are insanely long, tempers are flaring and people are getting into fights. I put my hand out and feel the sky grow in weight. It's about to come tumbling down on us all. Night comes we go to bed and try to forget all this. BBC 4 is full of laughs. Laughter is the antithesis of fate. Fate is a date with a rock and a steep hill. Fate is an interstate. Some go the way of Lear. Some Cordelia. Some Regan and Goneril. Some Edmund.

Some mad Tom. Some the Fool. The worst is not. So long as we can say, "This is the worst." And with that I'll shut my eyes and wait for tomorrow to rise.

As above so below. Below it bellows yellow balloons. Which rise. Watch them. You can see them in your mind. I'm converting the lead of everyday existence into a celestial slingshot. I see a being nothing there that is not unlike the sensation of being nothing here. Without you by my side. Please, take a load off and sit down. The rivers can flow by themselves. This isn't New Zealand. But it could be. We're all waiting to see what happens when you pull the plug on Australia. Not that I have anything against Australia. I've never been there, nor can I make the weather do things by putting words together. But I can make a kangaroo hop across my agenda in a Brook Brothers suit with a tie that has naked ladies on it. If you're willing to picture that, I'm more than willing to shout your name to the stars. Together we'll talk of Egyptian hieroglyphs in Renaissance art, and hit all the right bars. As above so below. A burning wind. A lost kangaroo.

Upon the shore of dread existence I found a strange yet beautiful food called music and scooped it up and brushed the sand off and ate it. And in this way I learned about pepper, and nebulas, and stoves. This is why change is so necessary, and bottles and grooves. And as the motorcyclists blasted along the coastal highway of Big Sur, the Pacific Ocean sighed, and slopped more music on the sand. It belched a whale, then receded with a soft blue hiss.

And this is how I discovered life. It had mechanical details and digested food. It was a cause of magnets and people kissing on couches. It consisted of divinities and bones. A pageantry of larynxes in which gravity played a role and oranges heaped one on another in grocery stores. We knew round from square and dazzle from drizzle but nothing about energy. We knew that it fed our engines and motivated boats and pushed our hypotheses to the brink of madness. Now I understand. To declare something to declare anything is to take a stance and risk hammers of criticism coming down on your head. There were glasses on the table and harmonies in the salt but is it reasonable to flirt with cemeteries? Some of my most beautiful thoughts occurred at the crack of dawn. No bodies were exhumed. It wasn't necessary. We adhered to a principle of syncopation which walked in beauty like the night. And shivered, barefoot on cold rocks.

What's more naïve than an olive? Maybe an apple, or a pear. What is the point of the question? Your honor, my client is a small oval fruit with a hard pit and bitter flesh, not an unschooled apostle entering Gethsemane for the first time. What we have here is a case of misrepresentation. Yes, metaphors are allowed here, the bigger the better. All correspondences are welcome. Life is a courtroom and we're on the stand twenty-four hours a day. The question isn't whether such and such a thing is true, but what aesthetics are in play, and what is the true nature of beauty. The olive is alive. And being alive makes it beautiful. Too pat? Too sentimental? So be it. But next time you encounter an olive, either as an hors d'oeuvre, or reposing in your martini, be respectful. No olive is naïve. The flavor has a bitter quality, and the fruit is fibrous. It is the perfect accompaniment to the subtleties of the social life, or the libidinal undercurrents of a cocktail lounge. If you're looking for something a little messier, sink your teeth into a peach. The olive is tart. It holds back. It encourages reserve. But the peach? The peach just lets it all happen.

I felt a stirring in my brain and wondered what it was. Was it my imagination looking for something to eat? Or was it a spoon of inquiry stirring a bowl of thought? Neurology is a voyage of interaction. It takes a lot of nerve. Does it help to know that the soul may or may not reside in the brain? The mind works through the brain but is separate from the brain. The mind uses the brain, stimulating Polynesia. I've attended enough funerals to know that had little to do with it. But memory is a strange and devious animal. And every third thought shall be my grave. What was I looking for? Nothing. I was looking for something once, but if I haven't found it by now, it's unlikely that it even exists. And what precisely was that? Precision has nothing to do with it. Introversion is a chain from which the mind breaks free and discovers propulsion. We all want the same thing. But it comes in wildly different forms. Mine was a slammed door, a jar of fireflies, and a ladder. When those things conjoined, I rested against the sky and ate a banana.

Bad air again today. 108 on the AQI index. Fires still raging in the Cascades.

There's been another mass shooting in Raleigh, North Carolina. Five dead, two injured.

Planet Earth is on fire.

The Rhine and Danube rivers are too low for ships to pass, paralyzing commerce.

Some things are hurrying into existence, and some things are hurrying out of it; and of that which is coming into existence part is already extinguished. Marcus Aurelius.

I was seized by an anamnesis, a memory of my life as a Viking. I worked all day at a forge making a sword. I hammered and hammered and hammered. Then I went out for some fish and chips at the Santa Monica Seafood Market on Wilshire. I get looks. Could be the helmet, but I think it's the berserker gleam in my eyes. This all began with Heidegger. I studied hammers. I studied hammers hard. I pounded the nails of knowledge into a pig iron brain. And this became a recording called Rivets of Predication. All based on a lie. It began with wood engraving and led to lithography. I became fascinated by fonts. Faith and skepticism and magic. And browsed the aisles at Goodwill looking for the truth. It hung there, full of intentions, so I tried it on. I felt an acute affection for calliopes and rocks. I went berserk. I slashed at the air with my words until a hole in the air opened bursting with light. And that's when I became a Santa Monica Viking.

I'm not a big Springsteen fan. But I do really like "I'm on Fire." Can't say what it is, exactly, the melody or the lyrics, the intensity of feeling or the line with the dull edgy knife cutting a six-inch valley through the middle of his skull. That's one hell of an image. I'm not a medical expert, but I'm pretty sure that would hurt. You'd probably have to wear a bandage on your head a long while, go around like a sheik in a turban. A sheik on fire. *Quod absurdum est.* And yet. Look at the sun: here you have a ball of fire. I feel its warmth in my body. The diffusion of that sweet energy in muscle blood and bone. Would you patent the sun, quipped Jonas Salk. Money is the devil's shit. Almost anything that happens in the sky is conferred with divine afflatus. Clear the runway. Taxi for takeoff. Now then. Let's talk about the spreading of differences among things. Let us rediscover the lost letter or the vanished sign, let us compose the dissonant scale, and we will gain strength in the world of spirits. Wrote Gérard de Nerval. First, fire and wood. Fire is fire. Wood is wood. Together they make heat and light. Take a word, take a world: together they make a squirrel. Turn a knob, open a door.

Light a stick of incense and hand it to a girl. Eyeliner and glitter aren't entirely convincing, but you can make some interesting friends that way.

Ecstasy doesn't come cheap. You get pushed there by a dozer of angst. Broken limbs broken heart the debris of a lifetime. And there you are, smiling out of a skull. Because the dam burst. Things went askew. Sparks flew. It's all a porridge ensconced in a cranium. This dome of neurons. This global bone. You get slapped silly by a rodeo of opinion. You go out of your head. Outside the circle. *Existanai phrenon*. If you could feel the weight of our coin jar, you'd know the metal of money already feels weirdly obsolete. Money has never been real. It's a narrative of credit, a fable of debt. Money borrowed from a future that drifts further into the future. But that's not ecstasy. That's imbecility. Ecstasy is sinking a shovel into the dirt and finding the meaning of roots. Intricacies of form mollified by snow. A face from the past frozen in ice, grinning.

The dirt is clean that brings life into the world. Wheat and corn and grass and barley. Hyacinths tulips lilies sunflowers roses. Dirt brings the bright out of the darkness of worms. Let this be my tribute to dirt. My slop my zipper my heat my engorgement to dirt. Hello friends I'm a jasmine. Performing an artful dance in a strip club in Vegas. I'm also the man oogling Lulu with a sweaty twenty-dollar bill in his hand. And this is another form of dirt, or what, for lack of a better word, we call dirty. Poor abused word. Dirt. The smell of it in a shovel when it's raining. When it's been raining. Long enough to soak in the loam and make it so fertile it makes the mouth water.

When I look inside I see outside and when I look outside I see inside. It's really just a matter of perspective, a turn of events,

and a weeping guitar. The ocean comes in a box. I pour pieces
of it onto the table. And begin to put them together. I do this
with all my perceptions. They shatter against my brain and come
raining down in a million different shapes and colors. Sometimes a fragrance will lure me into deep reflection and I'll bump
into the table. Or stub my toe on the magazine rack Jesus that
hurts I do it all the time I'm surprised I still have a toe. Life is a
puzzle we've all heard that one before. Well, it is. This is a piece
of it right here. The Beach Boys singing "Don't Worry" while
I worry if I'll still be here tomorrow. If any of us will be here
tomorrow. I'm not terribly good at accommodating death, but
it does get easier with age. I go for a walk, I look at things, I
digest them, process them, chop them into words where, by the
grace of language, they fill the void with auroras of stunning
anguished light.

Stuck inside again today. The AQI index is high, 155, unhealthy.
Our air purifier has been running all day. What a blessing to
have this device. Another wildfire broke out at Loch Katrine,
fifty miles from Seattle. The Bolt Creek fire is still going, as
are the White River fire and Minnow Ridge fire. No rain. No
wind. The smoke just floats above the city, a disconsolate,
ominous haze of forest destruction. I couldn't go out for a run so
I did some exercises indoors, including running in place, which
feels awkward, not the same as actual running, but it helps. I
listened to Hamlet on my earphones. Hamlet contemplating
suicide, "to be or not to be, that is the question." And yes, absolutely, that is the question. That's quite probably the most philosophical question anyone can ask. What is the value in continuing my life? When you consider the burdens, the thousand
natural shocks the flesh is heir to, bursitis, sciatica, psoriasis,
melanoma, fibromyalgia, muscular dystrophy, bad burns, gun-

shot wounds, punch to the solar plexus, the whips and scorns of time, outrageous hospital bills, cancel culture, censorship, dejection, rejection, impotence, betrayal, ridicule, fraud, disprized love, the law's delay, the insolence of office, which could all end in a minute with a bare bodkin, or a jump from a high bridge, or asphyxiation on a doorknob, *à la* Robin Williams. None of life's compensations seem to have occurred to Hamlet. A good meal, a bowl of ice cream, a glass of wine, a flowing conversation with friends around a fire, the euphoria of saving a life or helping someone out of debt, the satisfaction that comes with completing a hard task, writing a book, painting a masterpiece or reaching the summit of a mountain. Or just getting drunk. None of life's pleasures seem to have any meaning for him any longer. How weary, stale, flat and unprofitable seem to me all the uses of this world, he muses, jaded, sardonic, and disillusioned. What deters him is fear of an afterlife, which isn't surprising, considering the fact he's been visited by the ghost of his father. And thus the native hue of resolution is sicklied over with the pale cast of thought. Odd to think of thought as something diseased and unwholesome. But I agree, rumination is a source of depression. Abstractions remove us from the tangible and lead us into labyrinthine cerebrations that yearn for redemption but never find it. The lights flicker, the air is stale. The silence is deep. There's only the heavy breathing of the minotaur and the smacking of lips as he gnaws on the bones of his last victim.

I would like to have Thanksgiving with four robots. Joked comedian Tim Dillon. But I think he was serious. He was talking to an MIT guy, Lex Fridman, a computer scientist, artificial intelligence researcher, and podcast host. Robots aren't as weird and tedious as whacko family members, but how long would they live with me before they became a problem like me and I'd have to replace them? Adds Dillon. I get it. You wouldn't have to put up with a lot of blather from family members you only see once a year and whose banalities and toxic agendas test one's patience to the max. But how would robots be an improvement? How could a robot master the spontaneity of conversation, or have a sense of humor? Can humor be programmed? Isn't humor fundamentally illogical? A little crazy? How can you program a robot to be crazy? You'd have to know what crazy is and then find a formula for craziness. The essence of an image lies in the absence of the object depicted. Is that programmable? Could the polyurethane lips of a robot with obsidian eyes and a metal forehead respond meaningfully to a question about the feeling of exuberance in the George Harrison song "What Is Life?" On the other hand, wouldn't it be nice to program a robot to cook a turkey to perfection and bus the table and do the dishes and bring you a cannabis gummy on a silver plate? Without doubt, the saddest episode of *The Twilight Zone* was titled "The Lonely," based on a story by Rod Serling. A convict named Corry (Jack Warden) has been sentenced to fifty years of solitary confinement on an asteroid for a murder that Corry insists was committed in self-defense. Out of sympathy for his plight, the captain of the ship that brings Corry supplies and news from planet Earth four times per year brings him a robot in the perfect likeness of a woman named Alicia. The woman becomes an intimate companion. Several years pass. The ship makes a routine landing but this time the captain informs Corry that his case has been reviewed and he has been declared innocent. He may return to Earth, but only he can go, and must limit his baggage to fifteen lbs. This means he cannot bring Alicia. Corry argues passionately to find some way to bring her. He needs her. He loves her. The captain draws his gun and shoots Alicia in the face. She breaks down, malfunctioning, her face a mass of wire and broken circuitry, all while repeating the name Corry. Corry… Corry… Corry. The captain assures Corry the only real thing he'll be leaving behind is loneliness. Alicia wasn't real. She was a robot. "I must remember that," Corry mutters in an eerily neutral tone.

Writing drifts towards death. It does this by inflaming the magic of the image, which is a substitute for the real thing. However much you may debate the reality of the real thing, language exalts in the absence of things. It's the absence of things that gives language its soul. Its drive. Its purpose. Its blisters and lobsters. Its elaboration relations and deontic modality. Its evoked entities and ideophones and indirect objects. Language is the magic of folding. You can fold your arms you can fold a towel or a bedsheet, but when you fold one sound into another you're folding the essence of nothing, which is the linen of nothing, the sleeves of nothing, the pockets of nothing, and nothing is what it is, and why the language soars like music, its jealous twin.

The AQI was high today, just at the threshold between moderate and unhealthy. We decided, since we'd been cooped up in the apartment for two days, to risk going for a short combination walk and run around the crown of Queen Anne. We wore black N95 masks. It wasn't too bad, it didn't restrict my running much, just when I picked up speed or went uphill and I began breathing heavier did it become a problem to breathe. It was also quite warm, 83°. On our way back we saw a thick column of smoke to the east rise above Capitol Hill. That must've been the Loch Katrine fire. It's a Sunday, so there were a fair number of other people out for a walk. One couple brought a baby, leisurely strolling past us on the overlook of the Olympic Mountains, pushing the infant in a carriage, which I thought showed bad judgement. We stopped on the corner of Bigelow and Highland to whistle for Louise and her family to appear, which they did. They made quite a ruckus in the nearby trees. I think they were glad to see us. And Oriana's blue jay pal showed up, as always. She clipped Oriana's ear yesterday, out on the porch.

The moon fell out of the sky. I found it lying on the ground in Issaquah and rolled it home. It had quite a few dents in it. Or were those craters? The dust was soft as velvet and I could see the footprints where various astronauts had walked and jumped up and down and played golf. It wouldn't fit in our apartment so I left it at the end of the driveway and stuck a sign on it that said, "FREE." It was gone the next morning. Several weeks went by. It surprised me that nobody missed the moon. Was romance dead? Maybe the public lost interest after all those astronauts went there to play golf. No tides, either. No surf. Surfers sat in the sand, confused. Then, early last Monday morning, I received a postcard from the Smokin' Gun bar in Souris, North Dakota. It said: "Funny how drinking 8 cups of water a day seems impossible... but 8 beers & 7 shots in two hours go down like a fat kid on a seesaw." It was signed, "Yer pal, the Man in the Moon."

Much is made of what is inside and what is outside. Inside, we feel special. That's only natural. Inside, on a good day, the interior glitters like the Hall of Mirrors at the Palace of Versailles. On a bad day, the interior can resemble an M. C. Escher lithograph. You can get lost in a maze of corridors and staircases that revert back on themselves so deceptively you're not quite aware of what just happened, or how, despite the rigid geometric configuration, the structures seem to be obeying laws from the fourth dimension. People walk upside down or enjoy dinners on a vertical plane. It's a mathematical universe of ontic structural realism in which consciousness bounces around like a Slinky asking everything and solving nothing. Other modes of interiority can frame the exterior world in the mute inscrutability of iron or silver, or assume the prehistoric fecundity of a bayou in Louisiana where the eyes of alligators glow opalescent above the dark waters of the unconscious. This is how the intellect grabs what it can of the external world and builds thought and furniture out of it, or hangs metaphors like Christmas lights from a rickety sonnet. The interior feels immutably separate from the outside world, but the reality is just the opposite. There is no interior or exterior. The nervous system is no different than any other biological network. As for consciousness, no one knows what it is. That said, there's no reason to think it's unique, or that trees and plants are somehow outside the realm of consciousness when they're clearly not, or that they're outside of us at all, when it's apparent that they require the same sustenance as us, same water, same dirt, same air, same pizza deliveries, with the one exception being that their pizzas arrive in the form of sunlight, and have no topping, other than rain.

You can't use decimals except when you can. I learned this while swishing mouthwash. One had nothing to do with the other. One had everything to do with the other. But I can't solve this with decimals. I need to get plastered in a lizard lounge. There's a mathematics of the heart that bites the world with calculus. Objects extrude form the mouth in the form of words. In each word is another word and in that word is another word. And this is called infinity. Language is the Serengeti of infinity. Lions on a knoll thrilled with the sight of Paris. And this is called license. Like when we went to see Bob Dylan and I popped out and raced back to the house for my *Highway 61 Revisited* CD, and my driver's license, which I'd left in the back pocket of my other pants. Last night I went on a walk among the stars. I stopped to repair a radio and solve a riddle. The radio was tuned to classic rock. The riddle was tuned to life. I still can't solve it. Or even grab it. It happens too fast. And it's slippery as hell. I keep dropping it. And running after it up the hill.

On the way home from the Pot Shop, we decided to stop and get some hamburgers at Big Mac, on Queen Anne Avenue North. They were still closed for repairs after the upstairs apartment leaked into their kitchen, so we went to a casual restaurant down the street featuring pizza and pasta. I ordered the alfredo with meatballs and Oriana ordered the alfredo with chicken and a glass of wine. I asked for a root beer. Before Oriana had a chance to take a sip, a fruit fly got into it and was doing breaststrokes and butterflies. Oriana took it to the waitress behind the bar and asked for another, which our waitress graciously supplied. She also advised putting a napkin over the top of the glass. The door to the restaurant was wide open. It was a very warm day. A woman sat outside to have her dinner. She had arrived with a mask carefully positioned to cover the entirety of her face. Fewer and fewer people are continuing to wear masks. She reminded me of the soldiers after a war stationed in such remote places they haven't yet heard the war is over and years go by before someone tells them, or they die.

There's another side to this, of course, which is that the war is not over, the guns have dropped into the background, some of the troops have retreated, but now and then a bomb drops, or bullets riddle a grocery store, or a woman sits alone eating a calzone.

We left a large tip since the waitress had been gracious about replacing Oriana's wine. Unfortunately, the food had been disappointingly bland, almost the dead equivalent of airplane food. It was as if the chef had followed a corporate script rather than follow a recipe designed to enhance the flavor of the food. And I was still hungry when we left. It's getting harder and harder to find good restaurants. Those that Covid didn't kill, inflation and violence and decaying infrastructure have come close to finishing the job. Wall Street doesn't need the working class anymore to make their money. They have physicists creating bizarre, byzantine formulas for making money that is based on nothing. Nothing but debt. Debt is the new commodity, that and weaponry for war. The rest of us poor suckers with incomes well below the million dollar a year mark have been left to fend for ourselves. I first saw that with Katrina and New Orleans. Now it's Jackson, Mississippi, and Flint, Michigan, with no potable water for drinking or bathing.

I thought, not all that long ago, that we were lucky to be living in the Pacific Northwest, where temperatures would remain at a tolerable level and there would continue to be plentiful rain and water while other regions of the world baked into carcass and bone. Not so, alas. The AQI today from the wildfires to the east in the Cascades is 240. My being here is a bit of an accident. I was driven here from the Bay Area just when the first ominous signs of Silicon Valley emerged, rents began escalating and social gatherings began to turn high-tech and networked. I put all my worldly belongings into a Dodge Dart and went north. Grunge was at its zenith in the Pacific Northwest and rents were eminently affordable. Then Microsoft happened, and one by one the funky coffeehouses full of chess players and readers morphed into Starbucks and people ignoring one another with their laptops and cappuccinos. The poetry, however, remained surprisingly strong and resilient. It was always highly diverse, but now it was being fed the Cartesian abstractions of the then nascent tech industry, which decoupled it from empirical reality and disembodied it. The Bukowski wing sneered, then brought forth its antipodes of dark matter and barnacled pilings. The slop of green water. Smelt and starfish. And the smoke of opposition.

Our region's poetry — neon pinto, duck grating, sibilant iron — is more flatulent than the moldy marbling or phantom begonias found in the East Coast's decorous formaldehyde. In addition, the secretions bring strong dromedary wings of extremely intimate public display. The poem is a toy that falls from the hand like a rectangular courtyard. The words yield venison and fertilizer, but they can also knock down power lines and carry embers, spreading motels further. After thousands of years, Western poetry has adapted to the exigencies of disembodiment. Some poems have developed thick koans that are glued shut with a strong paradox. These poems need venues, attentive people with open minds and open hearts, which melt the restrictions of rationality, allowing the koans to open up and release seeds. These seeds then become grapes and reflect the world with which much twenty-first deformity is linked, paddling in desolation, gazing at the stars and groaning for a deity, which is so critical to the development of tread, and spitting ire.

What if you spilled your guts on a napkin, made a song out of it, got it on the radio where it went to number one with a bullet, would it be fair to say your endocrine system is pretty spectacular? My digestive organs don't produce much in the way of hit songs. But hey. They get things done. They pull nutrients out of the food I put in my mouth (where else am I going to put it?) and leave me full of warmth and sunshine. I'm not sure I can see that playing on a jukebox somewhere in the United States where they still have jukeboxes and 45s of Eddie Cochran and Etta James. And look at this, I can hold Kenward Elmslie's selected poems in one hand while I fold the interlibrary loan receipt with my other hand to make a more effective bookmark out of it. Roy Orbison rushes into the room and asks me if I have a song for him to sing. It's a ghost, of course. Roy passed away in December, 1988. Sure Roy. Here's one called "Can You Hear My Lizard Brain Bubbling Thoughts of You My Bouillabaisse Darling." And off he goes to a recording studio in the elsewhere. Sometimes a yearning can turn a midnight squalor into a soft blue glow.

I went to see a mystic who revealed to me all my past lives. In 1400 B.C. I was a locust in Egypt. I participated in a mob of gluttony which left Egypt at risk to famine and the Pharaoh vulnerable to sufferance. I was a microbe 3.7 billion years ago living in a rock. I had few opinions, no discarded cards, or a truck I could call my own, but I got my fill of methane. In 1876, while spending some time in Deadwood, South Dakota, I was holding a hand of aces and eights when I got shot in the back of the head by a man named Jack McCall. He was removed from my Christmas list. In 1347, in the precincts of London, England, I was a feisty *Yersinia pestis* participating in a pandemic called the Black Death. I remember rats and funny masks. It was hot when I was pulled into this current manifestation some years back in Minneapolis. It's never been quite clear to me why I'm here. Is this a mission? Do I have an objective? Apparently not.

Appearance rides on time and time is radically transitory. I wear it around the house like a nonspatial continuum with a pink bow and a ten-gallon hat. It's wonderful to discover a new poet. Particularly one that stands outside time and chews gum spiritedly in Time Square in the late 1950s. I would like to join you now in the predicate room. This is where all our nouns are manufactured. They are one part tin two parts copper and the rest is whatever meaning has crystalized in its core. When Keith Richards counts time it means he's about to slip into a warm gospel number. Time is on my side. Or at least I like to think it is. My relations with time have grown smoother with time. When it's snowing I feel simultaneously disappointed and joyful. It's hard to run in the snow, but I can do it, given enough time, and the proper traction. What I fear is black ice. That stuff can mess you up. There should be a song about black ice. Sung by a chorus of theoretical physicists. Eggplants. You know? They know everything there is about time. It's in their shape. They have certain properties. None of them tick, none of the tock. The time is right for a voyage into space. Send signals back to Earth. It's dark and cold here. I need more time.

Sometimes I listen to the chatter of the zeitgeist, or what one may call mainstream media, and try to see through its illusions. I was once captivated by them. But now, despite their manifest deceits, they seem a little sad. They're always trying to put lipstick on a skull. Or did I mean to say pig? Pig, skull, it's all the same in the end, this tired, tender ache which is all over you like a voluptuous feeling will one day turn a sour hour into a gown of railroad cars and indestructible transition, which is going on all the time, ephemera bouncing around in a stimulus, or a man on a swinging trapeze with his arms outstretched for your arms, assuming you have the imagination to extend them, and the inclination to do so, if this will help you to your muse, or mongrel instincts.

In a hot job market, showcasing the string of your guitar and investing in your tumescence is essential to steering away from statuesque conclusions. I've been hearing this all my life, hot job market this, hot job market that, as if the only thing in the world that mattered was chloroform. And it was all a lie. Except for the chloroform. Don't do what I did and jump in a river full of piranha and tedious little tourniquets for your toes. Feed your ambitions chocolate. Live large, like an alcoholic on a planet of beer. They say the best things in life are blatant. If I were you, I'd hurry on over to the table and get yourself some deviled eggs. I'd been a medical student for four years before I realized what to do with my kidneys. I loved them, and they loved me, and together we would try to be healthy, and compensate for the good times, which were sometimes toxic, sometimes intoxicating. Existence is an injury to the health we enjoyed in death. One of the greatest romances of surgery was the night I sewed the ghost of a clam to a candle flame and watched it correspond to the illuminations in my grimoire. Just what kind of surgeon are you, asked an old farmer out in his field one sunny afternoon. I dig up corpses and piece them together in a single being I shall call superman, I told him. He walked away shaking his head with a combination of disgust and incredulity. I think he already knew. A high temperature can lead to things like this. A man in a field wondering what to do with the heart in his hand.

You always say that you want to be free, but you'll come running back to me. Or so I thought 102 years ago. That's how it feels. The environment is so different now. Tornados, hurricanes, wildfires, mass killings, the threat of nuclear war, mass formation psychosis. Back in our day, we adults spent eons staring at a bolus of tinted wax inside a glass vessel which was stimulated by an incandescent light at the base to billow — like *pāhoehoe* — in languid undulations, and these were the lessons we absorbed, which were, admittedly, a little tedious after a while, and became the hum of a refrigerator, or brain. A little vapid at times, yes.

But then, we had Jimi Hendrix tearing the universe apart with his guitar. He was a voodoo priest lighting his guitar afire. The universe was reassembled by a toke of air. This was when it was fresh, and the sky was filled with UFOs. We loved the extraterrestrials and they loved us. We wondered if they existed and we wondered if they existed. And of course they did. And we did. Existence is easy. It's absence that hurts, that brings that exquisite anguish to the party, and quenches everything with dreams.

The idea that absence has a presence more present than absence itself has been proven time and again in the laboratories of the paragraph.

I like paragraphs. They are so big and lush, like a pupa. I like to think of a paragraph as a chrysalis. You unroll a sleeping bag of bronze afternoon and the smell of it tints your brain with the striations of birth. Streams rise to warm it into being. And I hold it like a cipher at the end of a string, a beautiful young woman in a bright yellow sweater dancing on a picnic table.

Sometimes the paragraph becomes an aquarium and the words come and go, wiggle a little from time to time and so engage the mind, bring it closer as the nerves worry their liquids and put a head of paper on a silver chest. The air is big at the border, and the road is awash with loops and minerals and what appears to be a mechanical gym shawl. Saturday is language's wall. It is glimpsed as sterling and spent like a drop of thunder on a recondite lover. Love is where the calories stick. It's subtle building soap, and ductile, like a Ben-Day dot in Dagwood. There is the scent of rice in the wind's furniture and the seep of hurry on a broken branch. Here the secrets are sympathetically painted green as they slowly unfold and skeins of abstraction light up.

It's a quiet place and if it doesn't go on too long it's a pleasure. And when it keeps going you know something serious is in the works. More words are required to pull hard at the stubbornness of thought and break the chain. Let the thing stand up. Let it show itself to the door and open it and walk into the casino, braced for calamity and whatever masterpiece gets thrown at your head.

A lot of people don't know this but Emily Dickinson was a bank robber. She put on a good disguise. A poet spinster holed up in her room, a profound disquiet in the presence of strangers. When, in fact, she was riding a powerful steed and robbing banks from Amherst to Agawam. She'd stride into the bank and say, "My life had stood — a loaded gun," and everybody would drop to the floor. She'd scoop the cash up from the tellers with terror in their eyes and swing up on her steed and take off in a cloud of dust. These adventures are what largely fueled her poetry. She didn't really care about the money. It was the adrenaline. The poetry of anguish, paid in keen and quivering ratio to the ecstasy of the whole thing, the gallop out of town, chased by the cavalry of woe. Back home she baked bread and seemed calm and smiled. Ecstasy defies imprisonment.

The AQI tonight is scary. 273, very unhealthy. A reading of twenty-eight more units for concentrations of particulate matter will put us in the hazardous zone. I hope our air purifier keeps working. Lord knows what the filter looks like. It's been running for days. It's all coming from the east. The Cascade range, normally dripping with rain this time of year, kids dressed up as skeletons.

"Fire crews cleared out fuels while others bulldozed and hand-cut containment lines. They also relied on and monitored existing barriers like roads, rivers and streams, to act as containment lines.

"Small planes and helicopters have intermittently dropped buckets of water on problem areas, Johnson said. The fire has mostly burned freely on the north side into the Wild Sky Wilderness.

"As the sun began to set Monday, Kris Pflugh of Chewack Wildfire was using a pickax to pull up hot ash and dirt, exposing orange embers. Beside him, Kenny Dickinson sprayed down the hot earth. They were mopping up hotspots as they made their way down Beckler River Road, north of Skykomish.

"Soon, crews like this one from Spokane, will get to go home. Officials hope the rain will subdue the fire until finally snow snuffs it out later in the year."
　　—Isabella Breda for the *Seattle Times*, October 19, 2022

I see the firefighters in France, who fight fires with a passion, a ferocity that matches the roar of the fire itself, and wonder what sage design there is to their strategy, as the aggressions of the fire go wild at night, radiating into the sky like the fingers of an insane deity. I've never had that experience, that devotion to conquering an entity so huge and overwhelming the trees crack and thud to the ground in abject defeat.

The crisis in which humanity finds itself — endless war compounded by the catastrophes linked to climate change — is one of tentative survival, wholly dependent on the caprices of a gas. It's an existential crisis, a crescendo of angst in the face of chaos. There's a weird thrill to it, the lifting of a veil of familiarity in which the reality of forces working in a manner that doesn't serve our interests has become cruelly vivid. I feel akin to it, it's what brought me into existence, but also outside it, alien to it, which may be a fault of culture, a moldy, anthropocentric view.

But what then am I? A thing which thinks.

A thing which doubts, tries to understand, conceives, affirms, denies, yearns, wishes, strategizes, defies, refuses, negates, squats, scrapes, scrawls, and can use a fork in the proper mode, pointing the tines down in the continental style.

I interact with a body and do what I can to satisfy its needs, give it food, slather it with soap and keep it clean, exercise it to prevent it from getting fat and frail and allow it repose when its muscles ache and — this above all — keep it dry and warm when it rains and the air bites shrewdly against the skin. Reproductive interactions come and go like snow. At first you're not sure if it's going to snow, you sense it, and then one by one a flake falls, and hours later the world is white and soft and uniform. Some form of magic has occurred. You don't know how it happened so that the formula may be repeated again, at will, and this is life, the errancy of it, and emporium.

In exchange for these services, my mind is given a room at the top in a spherical dome called a skull, two windows with which to view the world, a tongue with which to mold and chisel words, ears for hearing, and a nose for breathing and smelling.

Sensations are ephemeral as mosquitoes in Mukilteo, but when they rub shoulders with the muscle of knowledge, they agitate — wildly — like the flapping of a scarf.

When particles with one or another degree of spin interact with the nerves of the retina, they cause those nerves to jiggle in a certain way. This jiggling is conveyed to the brain where it affects the animal spirits, depositing these things into the brain where they lay around like puppets and stuffed animals until the mind stops rowing its ratatouille around in a never-ending circle and extends its annoyances into furrows of color. This causes light particles to spin into sensations of shape and jelly. The mind grows wide-eyed with wonder, catches a train of thought to New York City where all the museums are, and delicious Reuben sandwiches, and flickers like a hiatus high on medication. When the theater is closed, the mind (which has been asleep for some time now) is asked to leave, informs the body of these intentions, which is somewhat slow to apprehend them, and together they rise and make their exit into the world, where there's significantly less traffic due to the lateness of the hour, and philosophy in the sting of the air.

The problematic thus is: how does the stone come to remain the same as itself across its vanishing moments? How does it achieve "durative identity"?

I see it still, a stone, its indentations, the sharpness of its edges, its weight, and wonder how time and stone are preserved, considering the lateness of the hour, and many competing sensations, like the woman entering the cocktail lounge with a weary, discombobulated man at her side, whom she partially supports, until they can reach a cushioned bench and lets him go and the man flops down, semi-conscious. He is not a stone. He is stoned. These are two different things that go on in this circus we call time, but all are headed simultaneously toward an apotheosis of some kind, a flowering of realization or a nebulous emissary of honest opinions, and a gentle smile.

I'm mesmerized by the succinct suck of time, the way it recoils when the sun rises and bends the sky into highways and hills, horses galloping off in that random fissure we call a reverie, which splits the air apart and makes it initial the wall with its trellises and residue in the mind's eye. The wind lectures the hands that the investiture of time is romantic, considering the faucets of Sicily, the facets of Renaissance art and faces of prudent waiters who know when to interrupt a conversation is to not interrupt a conversation. There is a flow to things that time makes obvious, but how and why they linger in the mind is submerged in the warm film of the mind's reel.

Events occur and become memories and haunting dialogues and paint, flaking paint, newly applied coats of paint, which are always wonderful, and glisten in the mind where the mind's brush slathers a preserving lacquer over the breathing strings and woodwinds of the Brandenburg Concertos. I have an image of last spring, the umbrella opened like a wet bat with a ribcage of pale aluminum. That was when? The date is lost. Unimportant anyway. We've been in a drought. The entire world has been in a drought. Except for the places hit by monsoon and typhoon and cholera and diphtheria and *E. coli*. Ethiopia is rehabilitating wells and repairing pumps. If Rimbaud were still there, he'd be helping out. Or so I like think. And this converts rumination to speculation and slams the door on logic. If the mind is a theater, the ovations are sharply noted.

I was a little amazed to find the salt in the salt shaker clumped together from the moisture when I had difficulty shaking the salt out of it onto my scrambled eggs this morning. I took the lid off and rinsed it to clear the little holes and used a butter-knife to break up the clumps of salt. Today is the first day in a long while that the air was respirable again and free of the wild-fire pollutants and smoke that have been hanging like a deathly, apocalyptic shroud over Seattle. The windows in the bedroom were a mess, the grooves in which the windows slide back and forth full of gooey black mold, and water dripping down the window panes. This was caused by keeping our windows shut tight in an effort to keep the polluted air out. Our air purifier ran nonstop. The AQI was a whopping 273 yesterday. There has been little progress in containing the fires in the Cascades. The crews are poorly equipped and the prevailing strategy — a so-called "containment strategy" — means just letting the forests burn. This minimizes injury. I know something else that minimizes injury: being properly staffed and equipped. Thank goodness we finally got rain.

Acetaminophen, lovely word. I had some this morning, for a headache. I woke up to a wet furball on the floor and mold in the bedroom window. Life in Seattle is glue. It sticks to you. It's as hard to remove as a label on a plastic container of prescription drugs. It's not a city it's a diagnosis. One day a building walked into my head and I couldn't get it out. I rode the elevator to the top. I shook hands with the sky. And jumped. My chute opened like a paragraph, this paragraph, which even now descends to the sidewalk, where a falsetto sings "Chasing Cars," and a bus pulls to the side to pick up a group of people, most of them gazing at phones, and fold my chute and go home, where comfort awaits in the form of clean linen and tea. And acetaminophen.

Everyone is undercover these days. At least as much as one can be in a heavily surveilled society. If you can't be private, you can at least pretend to be private. Pretense is what you do when life becomes enchanted. Me, I'm the King of Onions. I weep all day and my tears become forget-me-knots. Rubies of sound issue from a nightingale. This my testimonial. It has a rich filling and an inscrutable crust. I don't know what it is. I have to call it something. The girl dancing naked in front of our table wants money. I don't even know what I'm doing here. Nobody told me fairyland was an ontological mistake. But whenever I turn the lights on a million elves dive under the appliances. And all my reactions are soaked in understatement.

I'm thinking of getting a Led Zeppelin T-shirt for our trip to Kauai. I'm not in the habit of wearing short-sleeved shirts. I don't like them. But I do like T-shirts. My favorite is the one with their first album cover on it, the Hindenburg in flames over Lakehurst, New Jersey, but it might not be such a good idea to display that one when I board the plane. There's a Hieronymus Bosch T-shirt but no one would feel safe sitting next to me. They'd be queasy and quiet the whole way, stealing a glance now and then at the knife blade between two giant ears or the hollowed-out torso with tree trunk arms. People tend to give you a little margin at my age, if they expect an eccentric, they'll get an eccentric, and political views that would make the dead scream from their graves. I wouldn't survive Twitter for a single day. Maybe I'll get the one with the Blake illustration, *The Reunion of the Soul and Body*, but what I really crave is Pollock's *The Deep*, with that deep black void behind a background of muci-laginous white. Me all over.

It rained today, a nice steady downpour. I went for a run. I won't say it felt good, it didn't, but in some way it did, there was a certain discomfort in the comfort of it, the normality of it as opposed to the unnaturalness of the drought and high tempera-tures, but also the genius of it, the genius of rain, which can be seen in the greenness it brings back in the grass, and the sparkle of it and the randomness of it. Longing for rain is a form of thirst, it is, of course, water, thirst is to be expected, but this is a weird thirst, the entire body yearns for rain, rain rain, real rain, because you can't duplicate the sensation by getting into a shower and running the water cold, which would be a disappointment. Rain is the milk of clouds, long teats of mist, the long division of steers, and big sacks of thunder. It's stunning to feel it like a dream, or a deepened understanding of just about anything. Everything is compelling in the rain, and sad like a song by Miles Davis. It's rare to see sparks in the rain, but the sparkles you see in glass spark shivers of the real.

Right around 3:00 P.M. or on a Saturday night Oriana made Greek Pasta, one of my favorite dishes, and we watched Bill Pullman sneak around in a fisherman's work area looking for clues, evidence of a human trafficking ring on an island off the New England coast. Season 4 of *The Sinner*. I find that title to be very New England. Sin is an obsession up north. The Puritans brought it. Before then, the coast was all moss and rocks and moose and fish. The spirits of the trees swayed back and forth. No good, no evil. Just wind and rain. And the demons of the forest.

I like dressing like a coal miner when I read. I put on a mining helmet with a built-in light bulb, coveralls, high visibility jacket and steel-toed shoes. It is then that I descend into the book. If the book is by Whitman, or Gary Snyder, I can find my way, for these are excellent guides, and who point to things and explain their nature and value. But if it's a book by Stephane Mallarmé, I must move slowly, and with caution, because I'm in the realm of the orphic, where nothing is linear but all is oblique, and novel, and strange. The floor is littered with string and bars of music. Metaphors can be assessed by their color, streak, luster, hardness or softness, illuminative power and specific gravity. Some have pungent, tumescent roots that play boisterously with the brain. Others are a weak glue that move on complex legs the color of silver. I once discovered a vein of ink that wrote itself into a shadow of meaning and mailed itself to the buttocks of a praying mantis. These labyrinthine galleries can be wearisome after a while. The underworld can be fatiguing. I recommend a long rest after these sessions, and taking a long hot shower to get the oracles out of the pores.

One is not necessarily really outside of time when we step into the zone of the poem. Sensations come and go and ride upon a time that exists in the cavity of the bone. If our position is firmly ensconced in the atemporal parameters of Now, that which appears in the Now is ever-changing, but Now qua Now does not change, the Now is not lodged in time, it's on the upper shelf in the back of the garage next to a gallon of Pennzoil. This has rather spectacular consequences for how we find ourselves disposed in existence. Imagine yourself seated at an organ in a recording studio. You're really not supposed to be there. The producer is freaking out behind the control board, but it's too late. The song has begun. "Once upon a time you dressed so fine, threw the bums a dime in your prime, didn't you?" You lag behind with clunky delays that sound great. You're outside of time, the organ knows this, the organ is warmed by the fire of your passion, and is placed where raw sensation greets the material world. How does it feel? It feels good.

I'm a bookworm. A nookworm. Tell me. What's a bookworm to do in an age of illiteracy? Join a Fahrenheit 451 club and start fires in the mind at night while sitting in a tent drinking hot tea? Spine and paper convulsing in silence. The rest is all mine, in some quite enigmatic way, not the words, no word is mine, it's not the words it's the speculations, the landscape, penumbras folding over the rattles in the boxcar, pepper on the stove, the whole idea of a boat gone crazy in your head. It's what we share with one another and the external world. What is mine is my personal experience of it. It is, one might say, Being's own paradox. For the way in which the word is experienced is always momentous in psychic life. Like that afternoon the Volkswagen my friend was driving got broadsided at an intersection and we went flying, time slowed way down, everything happened in slow motion, I could see my body rotating like an astronaut, and when it all stopped, and the car lay on its side, I thought that's it, that's what reading a book feels like when the writing is so engrossed in the value of syllables it breaks through to the other side.

A box explodes into the bristles of a hairbrush and I ponder the relevance of drugs. Do we need to be amazed by existence? Can we just ambush the next merchant that comes along and later, after we get a small fire going, sit around and discuss the history of liniment? The work we do crackles with excitement. I get tears when I think of that old bus to San Antonio. I wonder whatever became of linoleum. Do people still put that on their floors? I associate it with coffee and screen doors in the summer out on the prairie. It's thoughts like these that lead to throwing pillows at the wall. I can't even remember what I initially expected from life. I liked sitting close to a fire and hearing the thinnest, most delicate note on a violin I'd ever heard scintillate in the air. This was followed by a lot of drums. This is what Beethoven does. He fills everything with space. And then lights it on fire with a baton.

The adherence stick is helter-skelter. Echoes purify the shout. It came from a rock. A rock is a box of fossil. Ancestry has wives. I feel haunted by the coast. We can barely see it. We've been floating here all night absorbed in repentance and amber. Perception turns into grace. You must be patient. Or somebody might crawl out of your ear and shine the next breeze to breeze by. The gargoyles are all stationed in southern Mississippi. The music there is blue. And so transparent you can hear a phonograph in it. The Beatles at the Hollywood Bowl. Throwing new ideas into the mind of the universe. You can see it in every face. The gratification of seeing a music created by a new outlook. My cousin is an iconoclast in prayer. I'm a refugee with a jukebox education and a flair for urgency. Just wait and see. Every repro-bation begins with a little sugar. And a good word bent sideways so that it inclines to action. Real love the kind that you need. Pieces of fruit and rind boxing the validity of words. Potentially communicable as pesos.

It requires a lot of Beethoven to drown out the noise of the upstairs neighbor making dinner. And when I say making, I mean making: heavy equipment is involved, actual machinery, sawing, pounding, hammering, drilling, sanding, polishing, welding, riveting, and metal injection molding. I have no idea what kind of food requires this kind of industrial approach, sheet metal sandwiches maybe, or potato salad propulsion sys-tems for orbital maneuvering in a one-bedroom apartment. I'm just reporting on the variety of noises involved. Thank God for Bose earphones.

Beethoven didn't work out. There are too many quiet moments. He likes quiet, gentle little sounds interrupted by storm and bluster. I turned to Bach. He fills a space with such a variety of sound there are rarely any quiet interludes. Beethoven is prodi-gal. Bach is tropical.

Jimi Hendrix would be perfect, but I can't find much of his work on YouTube, and his music makes a gymnasium out of my head. Words turn rogue and invade Venice dressed in tutus and Phoenician lobster bulbs while beetles tap dance on the skulls of dead musicians. These are imaginary constructions, self-indulgent linguistic perversions, but I have to feed them something. So I feed them apocalyptic crackers and syntax. It's a small price to pay for peace and quiet.

Do words transform things? I mean, can they? Can words alter reality? Like that guy, Prospero, creating storms and banquets out of air. Thin air. I dislike the name of our state. Washington. How dull. But does the dullness of the name alter the state of its statehood? No, it doesn't. No connection. The names of its counties and cities and towns are quite another matter. Wenatchee, Yakima, Walla Walla. Skykomish, Chumstick, Puyallup. Cle Elum, Kittitas, Lilliwaup. These are words derived from the Coast Salish, Chinook, Cowlitz and Lushootseed languages. When I hear them I think of mud and water, rivers, estuaries, swamps, ponds, inlets, coves and mountain creeks. The smell of the shore when the tide goes out, mucky, sticky, visceral. A rubber boot getting pulled off by the suck of muck near an oyster farm. A cold wet bough of Douglas fir brushing the skin of your face. These are all in the names. Muddy evocations calculated on the nerves of a hummingbird. What formulas or incantations can you make of these things that will in any way alter the determinations of the world? I don't know. I'm still experimenting. I'm building a totem of languages that will rival the tower of Babylon. And this is the language of horseshit. Which is the magic of the epithet. There's as much leverage in that as in the breath of a squirrel. Which, according to the butterfly effect, just became a fitness franchise in West Texas.

Here's a word for you: Iceni. Are you familiar with the Iceni? The Iceni were a Brittonic tribe living in southeastern Britain during the Iron Age. They battled and made treaties with the Romans and lived in roundhouses of clay and straw. They were a

Germanic speaking people but their language had resemblances to Celtic Welsh. They minted coins of gold depicting animals such as wolves and birds and human faces, animals on one side, human faces on the other. The Iceni were adept at hand-to-hand combat and painted their bodies with woad, a flowering plant of the mustard family. Boudica, Queen of the Iceni, led a revolt against the Romans, who had whipped her and raped her daughters, still in their childhood, in front of her, after her husband King Prasutagus died. The battles made a bloody mess of the Roman legions until they encountered Suetonius who, though vastly outnumbered, won by employing a superior strategy.

Oriana comes to tell me that it's 88 degrees in Kauai today. We'll be going there in a little more than a month. Five weeks. We're ambivalent about it. Neither of us enjoy traveling that much, we're shameless homebodies, but we needed to do something with the airline tickets she received when she retired, a very generous gift from her employers. We mainly worry about Molly, our cat. Who, at this very moment, is warming my thigh with her body, curled there as always in the evening. I wish I could communicate with her telepathically. She needs to know that when we've gone missing for those four days, we'll be back. Of course, if threats of nuclear war keep getting bandied about by depraved, infantile, insane world leaders, we may not make it to Kauai at all. The Clutterbuck administration seems to have a hard-on for nuclear war.

At night we listen to comedy shows on BBC 4 Extra until we fall asleep. The weather has finally begun to change. It's resembling winter now. The air is cold and invigorating. The wildfire smoke has been dispelled. A steady day-by-day rain has been expunging the wildfires.

In the morning, it's nice to walk into a warm living room and have Oriana at home drawing, reading, doing French exercises and enjoying her newfound leisure.

We go for a walk. The light on the lake is thin. It flirts with the docks and disfigures the water.

New doesn't happen to me often. I'm not sure how I feel about this. I'm so accustomed to being old that I tend to see everything as old. Except food. Our food is new. We discovered something new about food tonight. Oriana got an app for a food delivery service called Ouroboros. We ordered dinner from a local teriyaki restaurant that specializes in delivery. After Oriana worked out the details and sent the request I settled back expecting a wait of fifteen or twenty minutes, quite possibly longer. But no. Seconds later the guy was here. Oriana went out to greet him and get our meal, which had already been paid for, including a tip. This is new. And quite amazing. These services have been truly accelerated after the pandemic. Talk about paradigm shifts. This is one of the better ones. Tremors in the fabric of daily life tend more usually to be demoralizing and discombobulating, but this one is nice. The rest of the evening was modern, indelible, and kind.

I'm full of adjectives tonight but I don't know if I've got the energy to airlift them to safety. The nouns around here can get rough. Especially the hairy ones with fangs and appetites. Nouns like cloak and factory. The mesh of gears in the commission of thought. I get listless just thinking about the principles involved. If you mismanage a rhododendron, the entire universe weeps. It doesn't require much. Just a few kind words, a tropical architecture, and a sprinkling of tongues.

Lately, I've begun feeling a deep sadness whenever I look at my books. This is not the world for which they were intended. They're as good as museum pieces representing a bygone era. This is not a time of reflection, of subtlety of thought or openness of mind. The times are barbaric. The babble of celebrities far exceeds the mutterings of a wise old man in a chair by the window. But I've known this for some time and it didn't seem to bother me as much. For a few years people would gaze admiringly at them. I'd even have to worry about the inevitable request to borrow one. It pained me to lend books. I'd never see them again. So I learned French. Half my library is in French. Loaning books, meanwhile, has long since been a problem. It ceased being a problem at the beginning of the new century. Right around the time I started getting obsessed with poet Lew Welch. He felt it too. This poisonous obsolescence. For which there's no cure but more immersion, a defiance in which the flutter of paper whispers light utterances on your face.

I often feel like a monk circa 793 A.D. gazing out of a window at Lindisfarne and seeing a Viking ship land ashore and the men getting out, a glint of light on a sword and wondering what the fuck, what are those shits up to.

See what I mean? The interface between sensation and image is a transitional zone where the actual, swarming materium of life becomes visceral. One must curve up and down like a wave if one is to expect anything to come of potash, or postulation. Step back, and watch it explode into handsprings.

"Magic is ontological: it works through the propagation and reception of belief. *For I will come to perceive what I believe to be true.*

"Or try it this way: All belief is magic; image is its instrument. Image imposes itself between vanishing sense and constant concept; between the radical transiency of momentary time and the quasi-atemporal presence of thought and its power to enunciate the appearance of a world."

> —Charles Stein, "The Watch-House Where the Switches Keep: A Configurative Ontology of the Image"

At night, alone on the bed, I attract a stew dance, a seminal bombard of dribbling Byzantine kings glowing in a promenade. Travel floats my personality over a crystalizing pond. Lucidity swings into occurrence and creates a new set of collar studs. The green jungle takes shape. A painting in the municipal museum punches morality in the jaw. Golden coins spill from the mouth of a naked Titan. A hot broken symptom of late capitalism has been placed on a plate of Adriatic sturgeon. This is it, folks. The beginning of the end. The end of the beginning. The furtive enigma that carried me into this bar is circulating a rare form of pickle. Everyone can smell it. Heads turn. Tears well in a face of wide-eyed oblivion. I ambush a quivering twig of meaning and feel a spectral French ocher rivet itself to a new aesthetic based on horticulture. Mosquitos bleed invention. This is precisely what language does. It drives a melee to the border of Bohemia in the loving scorpion night and plants an orchid on the moon. I get dressed in the fervent balm of failure. The grid is down. The night is quiet. A street tarp flaps in the wind.

I needed to go to Big Five in Ballard and buy some new running shoes. Oriana asked if we could also take our electronic refuse to a recycling depository. I wasn't too keen on adding that to our schedule, since neither of us were sure of where this place was, and I hate driving in Fremont, it's one of the most confusing districts in Seattle, which is chock-a-block with confusing districts, but I agreed. I took the printer, which had expired a few weeks back and was taking up space on a small glazed coffee table with one of my father's watercolors beneath the glass, next to Oriana's Christmas cactus, enriched and mellowed by a full spectrum grow light bulb, and Oriana collected all the electronic detritus in the hallway and loaded it into the car. We found the right address for the recycling depository but no sign or indication that it was in the building. Oriana found a phone number for the place and was given a number to dial on a security box outside which opened the door for us. We found a listing on the building directory and rode the elevator to the second floor and found the room and knocked. A large shy bearded man opened the door and pointed to a big pile of electronic gadgetry piled on the floor. It seemed like a very strange use of office space, but we added our junk to the pile and left.

At Big Five, I found a pair of Saucony Grid Raptor running shoes, tried on a size 12 (my actual size is 10 but in the past few years shoe measurements have varied drastically) and it felt great. I asked if they had any luggage straps, I needed one for the carrying case for my Bose earphones I'd just ordered through Amazon, but it hadn't come with a strap. The guy — a very friendly man who reminded me of Popeye — checked a spot where they might've been, or would've been, if they carried any, but they didn't. He suggested Fred Myers.

We checked at Fred Myers, but they didn't have any either. We bought a strawberry cake and returned home, where I ordered a strap on Amazon. It's now such a strange, dysfunctional world that it has become infinitely easier to shop online than go to a store. I prefer going to actual brick and mortar stores — you can get a look at things before you buy it, try things on, get a physical feel for the product, etc. — but store inventories run from pathetic to you've-got-to-be-kidding.

The bookstores are the saddest places. I don't go in them anymore. It's too demoralizing. The evisceration is most noticeable in the larger stores, where the books have been rendered superfluous compared to the other merchandise, quite often touristy tchotchke.

The weirdest places are electronics stores, the few remaining ones, usually a franchise struggling to keep going at one of many malls that are also struggling, and where most of the other stores are already gone. Electronics are especially difficult to find since there are so many specifications involved and finding compatible parts is crucial, but now it's nigh to impossible. A lot of the shelves are empty and — to judge by the layers of dust — have been so for a long time. And when I ask for the item, I always get the same answer: we can order one for you. At which point I have to inform them that the whole reason I came to the store is so I wouldn't have to order one. I used to get that at the bookstores, when I was still foolish enough to think they might carry an obscure author such as Samuel Beckett or Saul Bellow, "we can order a copy for you."

Later, when the dust settles, it's swell to feel some poetry arrive and swell into palpable form, nipples and chandeliers. I neglect to bang around and just get up and go. I shake all over like a door in a hurricane and hook a moment of dazzling marmalade with my Crazy Jane cane. It's benevolent to suggest a coat. Some people find it healing and light in calories. I would include sidewalks if it helped in any way to augment the pleasure a sense of realism can bring to an arena of hypnopompic gauze. It's easy to buy reading glasses, but it can feel overwhelmingly anonymous, and bronze and visionary all at once. Feeling is lyrical. This is why it opens like a flower rather than a language, which is more like fish, Nile tilapia and iridescent shark. I can make a chestnut talk, but not a piece of chalk. Chalk has its own special power, which may be seen making paradigms striate on a blackboard. For example, once my stomach drank a staircase and I didn't find out about it until a man walked out of my mouth looking for Machu Picchu.

It's true, I don't much care for Proust's aristocrats, nor for all the social gatherings, what gets me hooked on reading this guy are the many subtleties of mood and consciousness, a knack for combining architecture and landscapes with the language, and do it so deftly, that you can't see where the landscape leaves off and the language begins, they become one and the same, and the ultimate disappointment to all this, as Proust finds out again and again, is how the illusions created by language seem paradoxically more real and enchanted than the reality, which always falls flat. I can relate to that. The imagination is always more perplexingly ancient than night, and its stars are made of life-affirming bedsprings forged in genuine Tijuana syrup. You know what I mean. If it looks back at you and grins, give it a hug. Just don't look back when you leave.

It's easy to affirm a banana. But you do have to know what you're doing. You can eat it. Eating is a form of affirmation. But eating makes things disappear. Which is, in essence, a negative. You can write an ode to a banana and do a reading full of enthusiasm, but you run the risk of sounding cute and affected. These things always end up sounding witty while the reality scampers off like a scared rabbit. Nor is affirmation uniformly a celebratory event. Affirmation can be neutral. You can affirm that the soil of Mars comes from weathered volcanic rock and that it has clay and silt-sized particles, but mostly it's just sand. The reddish color is because it contains a lot of iron oxides, or rust. And it will not grow bananas. Enthusiasm (the word means to be inspired or possessed by a god) does help convey a compelling affirmation. The need to affirm things comes from a very deep place, a misty fjord of divination full of crags and ice, not unlike the Pauli exclusion principle, which states that no two electrons in the same atom can have identical values for all four of their quantum numbers. In other words, no more than two electrons can occupy the same banana, and two electrons in the same banana must have opposite spins. You can take the amplitude out of a probability but you can't take a probability out of a drumstick. An ecstasy may be launched on a Wednesday and still require a spine of vertebral velvet to do the monster mash. This proves nothing, but it's pretty to think about. Who doesn't like Tallahassee at night? It's an emotion to be elected, but humming is recommended for pretending to a soapy languor. And that's when I saw it: a wad of gum by the haberdashery still.

I ended my affair with the banana some time ago. I'm into scrambled eggs now. I like to watch the goop — albumin and yolk — congeal into a curdled meal. Sound congeal into meaning. Gusto relax into gluttony.

It's amazing how soft some sounds can be. Fog, obviously, must be excluded. It's too loud. I can hear it clank down the street with its bag of agates and its buttermilk neurons. I'm in a state of distress over this business. The foliage in our experiment was a lovely anomaly. A rhododendron ate two children. When it vomited them up later, they'd become adults. I was born the only child of a melee of scarves. My father was a melee and my mother was a scarf. I never really got to know them, I was raised by a rose until I was twelve, and then I became first mate on a brigantine called the *Ferdinand Pessoa*. We sailed under the stars and dozed in our hammocks during the day. I pinned a piece of gum to my body in a heavy cold room for luck, which was delivered to me years later by truck and came wrapped in a ball of lightning. I wrestled a chrome ear on the bone mat and set a sequel of poetry on fire. It burned down the English language and left everything in ruins. And that's when people began to talk again. They rubbed their legs like crickets and created democracy and eggnog. I've always had a fondness for filigree. It cries for the monasteries, which are a little bedraggled in places, but dazzling to the noses of Madrid. I extended a moment of black into a pool of liquid time and felt the night roll back from the dawn. And this engulfed me, and made me loud like the fog, crashing through the fjords of Andalusia.

I wonder if there's a way to resurrect the film industry. Jettison the word *industry* for starters. I think I'll start by growing some feathers. And a pair of celluloid eyebrows. Then wave an enormous wand over Hollywood from the knoll of Griffith Park. Where I shall also greet the first extraterrestrials to bother coming here to see if there's anything they can do to resurrect the film industry. That word again: *industry*. Get out of here, industry! I see a film in which Nicolas Cage becomes a mad nuclear physicist and reinvents pudding. The pudding is full of nuclear fusion and starts a rebellion against structure. The pudding becomes a sensorium imposed through public media in the hope of inducing a more viable ontological orientation in the very moment of beholding it, or of producing it infra-psychically. In other words, transformation in appearance taken as transformation in substance, which is the very essence of pudding. Gene Hackman comes out of retirement to play the Emperor of Pudding. He grows mad with power and invades Ohio. He and

Nicolas Cage duel with Shakespearean sonnets in a Cincinnati junkyard. Tom Cruise emerges from a cocoon of cellophane in the middle of our kitchen and makes us popcorn, a well-known ally of pudding. NASA, with the aid of Samuel Jackson, sends a robot into space in search of a plot. All the good plots have been used. We need a plot for pudding. No plot, no pudding. No pudding, no plot. Catherine Deneuve is the sly visionary who descends in a silken gown to liberate Hollywood from the grip of adolescence. I don't think this is leading us anywhere. In fact, I'm sure of it. This isn't leading us anywhere. And why would it? It's just pudding.

Elsewhere in the world, it's not so much a matter of pudding than footing. Mine has begun feeling shaky lately.

The president is playing chicken with Russia. Not to mention China.

"Despite progress in reducing nuclear weapon arsenals since the Cold War, the world's combined inventory of nuclear warheads remains at a very high level: nine countries possessed roughly 12,700 warheads as of early 2022. Approximately ninety per-cent of all nuclear warheads are owned by Russia and the United States, who each have around 4,000 warheads in their military stockpiles; no other nuclear-armed state sees a need for more than a few hundred nuclear weapons for national security."
    —Federation of American Scientists

It's a remarkable feat when you think about it, to imagine anoth-er reality. One that previously existed, or never existed at all. I can see Van Gogh in a cornfield, or Brigitte Bardot lying naked on her stomach in an unmade bed. A Viking ship in a North Sea fog. Ulf, the son of Ivar, taking a piss at the stern. Tarzan riding a pterodactyl over Geryon Montes on Mars. A red-headed man chiseling name and date on a tombstone. How are these things possible? How odd to have this magic in your head and still be able to do the dishes. Or play a guitar. Or chisel a name. And how odd that one's fate can be linked to the infantile, moronic, and reckless behavior of politicians and generals. Who wouldn't want to be Superman? And drop kick these idiots into outer space.

As you can see, I'm crumpling a noise to caress it into a baritone. Then I'm going to fold the experience of piracy and put it in the drawer with my socks. I feel like a letter in a parachute. So I scratch an emissary neuron and feed the pavement a hill. There's a cold lake in the windshield. Avoid the ignition equation. It doesn't work right. It's beginning to show signs of mawkishness. I move away from the dark grimacing. It's not easy to feed a diary shreds of your life wrapped in tea leaves. The fuchsia is a phenomenal tree. Although it's not a tree. It's a rear admiral in the garden of folklore. I was there on Wednesday. I had an appointment with an ocean. When the night fills with propane you know there's something up. Ancestry comes in many guises. When I discovered I was related to the tomato clownfish I became stern and ruled the world with my fins. You're not going to find much logic in this aquarium. But don't worry baby. Sip some bourbon and smile. We've got fifty miles to go and there's a hot station on the AM dial.

The Good (remember the Good?) has no form and is logically ineffable. Which is why I love it. One cannot attribute properties to it. Fat, thin, heavy, light. Hard, soft, thoracic, Jurassic, lilac. You can't see it, taste it, smell it, hold it, hug it, drink it, eat it, or sleep with it. That's what makes it so damn good. What makes the Good so goddamned good. The formlessness of the Good expresses its rain in the grain and grass of the phenomenal. Its reign and variability in the surrounding hills and valleys. The forms of the world arise in this process and urge understanding. There's no phanopoiesis without sentience. The night's the time for all your tears. Your heart may be broken tonight. But tomorrow in the morning light. Don't let the sun catch you cryin'. This would be something of an embarrassment for everyone involved. Sunlight doesn't come easily. It must be milked from oblivion. Things come to settle gradually in the unconscious. The silt there is so fine that even symbols get lost. The intellect gives off a scent like late summer in West Virginia. And nothing mechanical gets in the way of emigration. You can leave whenever you want. But returning is out of the question. You'll be changed. The world will be different. The world will be speedboats skimming the water. And this will be good.

Oriana enters the room to tell me there have been signs that Mauna Loa may erupt in the near future. Thirty-six earthquakes have occurred in the last few days. It is surmised that the unrest causing the quakes is being driven by the renewed input of magma two to five miles beneath the volcano's summit. Its last eruption was in April 1984, thirty-eight years ago. We worry that if it erupts near to the date we're scheduled to fly to Kauai, air flights may be disrupted by all the ash and particulate in the air, as happened in March 2010, when the Icelandic volcano Eyjafjallajökull erupted. And what would happen if Mauna Loa erupts when we're in Kauai? How would we get home? We worry about Molly, our cat. She's never been left alone since we got her at an animal shelter seven years ago.

I do look forward to walking out of the November calendar back into the warm embrace of summer. We're not just making a significant geographical alteration in our future — a sybaritic dislocation of four days — but going outside of time as well, since Seattle will be fully submerged in the gloom and cold of winter when we exit the plane in Kauai into eighty-some degrees of tropical warmth. I should go buy a colorful short-sleeved shirt. There are no tropical vestments in my wardrobe. I dress like a cowboy most of the time, even though I don't herd cattle. I herd words. I'd dress like Marcel Proust if I had the money. And lived in Paris. Which I don't.

Added to the worry of Mauna Loa, is the much more serious worry of nuclear annihilation. There's been an escalating trend in talking about the possibility of nuclear war. It doesn't just make you feel impotent, it makes life feel cheap. There's no reverence for life whatever. The people doing the saber-rattling are depraved addicts of war, and the astronomical amounts of money generated by war. I feel the iron of a cynical sadness. I'm sauerkraut. I'm ground paper. I feel the ooze of theater flow over me in a nauseating mass of brainwashing propaganda. I turn to language for its illusions of power. The same words that bring us misinformation and the poison of propaganda can also be used to kick the doors open. I can lick the meringue algebra of the supramundane, feel the undulation of fins in the syntax of the surrounding foliage. Hear the wind in the poplars, calculate the exhilaration of Friday night with a case of congratulatory red. The high green beak of significance displays a wind-like watermark. I feel the effulgence of proposal lift itself like a Komodo dragon and move toward the edge of reality. The regatta spreads itself all the way to the horizon. A bird of indigo flaps its wings and rises toward the moon.

It's 6:37 P.M., October 31st, Halloween. Earlier, we walked around the top of Queen Anne Hill and noted all the tombstones and skulls and skeletons adorning people's lawns, including a mariachi band and a flock of skeletal flamingos. The crows were numerous. They turn fiendish for peanuts this time of year. I'll frequently hear the inimitable sound of their wings passing near to my head, almost like the sound of a woman's silk gown. What kind of world is this where death is mocked and celebrated? Well, why not? What else is there to do with death? It won't bounce like a basketball. Death is only a word. Until I die I won't know what the fuck it truly is. I do know people disappear, and disappear for good. I'd love to see a ghost. There'd be proof, first of all, that there is, indeed, a further existence after death, though I can't imagine how strange that would be, to have a numinous existence, a sense of self, but no body to contain it. According to Swedenborg, every person living on earth is already in contact with angels and evil spirits, even if we don't realize it. This awareness, for lack of a better word, most often comes in the form of a stray thought or impulse disguised as our own inner voice. That's pretty vague. I'm not sure how to deal with this information, jettison it as worthless (I won't) or try and ponder it, persist in exploring it until it asserts enough of its own reality to hold our attention and become — in some fashion — real. Swedenborg cautions against speaking with ghosts. I mean, look at Hamlet. That didn't go well. Swedenborg warns that some of the spirits out there are evil. You really don't want to engage with those. He also emphasized — and this is welcome news — that the Divine is stronger than any evil influence. He also said that things in heaven are more real than things that are in the real world. Which would include, no doubt, a lawn adorned with skeletal flamingos and a mariachi band whose songs cannot be heard, except by the dead.

Enchantment begins with the platypus. The platypus is semi-aquatic. It's versatile. Flexibility is an offshoot of music.

Jazz improvisation. Feudalism is just plain grotesque. Ask any-one with a virtual reality helmet on their head. You can hang a room with beautiful sounds, but has a flower been created, or a new language for describing the rain on the Champs-Elysées? The universe is only real when it crashes into satire. Collisions in a hadron particle accelerator. When it breaks apart, fragments may be scrutinized. The needling of the unknown, the clink of ice in a glass, the rippling of sand on a Saharan dune. I was feeling shy and so sat in the back of the revival meeting. We were trying to revive perception from the sterility of digitalization. And when the climate switches to redemption we can all enjoy the flexibility of yellow and find an old stamp to put on the letter we've written to the souls of heaven. Particles carry more information than we can detect. Inherent randomness is at the crux of everything. But don't be too rash. Sometimes it's a good thing to plan ahead. Check the depth of the water before you do a backflip off a cliff in Montenegro. Sit down and spend some time talking to the navigator and captain. The easy bones of the hummingbird are a lesson in hesitation. We're in a dif-ferent world now, one that offers heavy metal bands an excuse for their braggadocio. Remember last Easter in Monaco? There were hidden variables to consider, orioles and contraltos whose interrelationships turned prickly with relativity. Postmodernism upsets a lot of people. It gets blamed for a lot of social dysfunc-tions. The relativization of everything. But that's not the fault of postmodernism. It's the scarlet membrane of fate, the drop of grapefruit squirted in your eye at breakfast.

I like dumplings. But I don't like ants in my soup. No matter. Don't look now, but the lava is getting closer. We'd better get going. Here: take my guitar. Think of it as a genital. A big one, but completely harmless. Look at the way sunlight penetrates the wings of this wasp. The radiance of a veined transparency is greater than a word, but similar. The difference is in the texture, the magnetism and friction, the argument each makes. Some things resist interpretation. They're made of a language as yet unspoken, unheard, unwritten, unborn. This is the job of the poet. To provide speech for these things. It's all in understanding, perception, level of awareness and the amphibious pencil case on your lap. As you can see, it's growing. It must like you.

The diver doesn't feel the storm above, the crashing waves and tumult. The calm is deep. Whatever dangers lurk there are silent. The key to a successful voyage isn't catharsis, it's mirrors. Illusions feed on illusions. You can sell the wind as it wavers, but you can't sell waves. Waves aren't things, they're manifestations of energy. The chasm is seminal to the embalmment of books. If you see a woman in a kitchen smashing ginger with a wooden mallet, the issue isn't immaterial. You must get things done quickly or live forever in a hypothesis. Hold your belt buckle while you walk into the room. You don't want your pants sliding down. There's nothing hypothetical about walking. It's all about falling forward as if a strong wind were at your back. This convinces people you have a mission. Do you? Are you consumed by a persistent yet inchoate goal that draws you into the future like a seductive scent? My mission is simple: dig the magic of indolence. I can sit in a boat and stare at jellyfish forever. This is the magic of the gaze. You must undertake to furnish your life with age. Let it hang like sauerkraut from a skull of glass. The carpenter has everything at stake. He keeps walking around with a bag of nails. I think there's music in there. And if it isn't, you can affirm it with a hammer and ten thousand pills.

8:15 P.M. Tuesday. The news in France tonight disquieting as usual. The flora and fauna in the depths of the Mediterranean are dying due to unprecedentedly warm temperatures. Kiwis are being harvested much later than usual. There are water wars in the commune Sainte-Soline, in the Deux-Sèvre department. People are protesting the use of mega-basins for the use of irrigating crops — chiefly corn — because of the ecological damage they cause. Environmentalists say the mega-basins damage valuable wetland areas that provide habitat for a wide variety of wildlife. The area is also known for its salt marshes that produce a highly prized *fleur de sel*. Protesters also say that the mega-basins draw water from groundwater reservoirs which makes the droughts worse for local residents and smaller farmers, who see the basins as a "water theft" from locals by big-agribusinesses. Sixty-one gendarmes have been seriously wounded.

I watch the news in France because I can't take the U.S. mainstream media. Too painful. Too much propaganda, misinformation, nincompoopery, deceit, careerism and melodrama. The French news isn't all that much better, but discussions are far more vigorous, there's far more variety, and this diffuses — and defuses — the propaganda. Most of their struggles are identical to ours — same climate change catastrophes, rise in violence, crime, economic hardship, and never-ending war. But since France has a parliamentary system of government, they're more tolerant of multiple views. They don't have the same infantile tribalism that exists in the States. They're not as easily fooled by personalities. They focus on substantive issues. They're not as obsessed by celebrities. They love their celebrities, but they don't confuse their celebrities with celestial beings. They love them for their art, not an artless vulgarity. When their elites get too predatory and arrogant, they chop their heads off. Or at least they used to. They've backed off a little on that front. But when they get pissed, they get loud. The women don't wear pussy hats and the men don't grunt inarticulately.

8:14 P.M. Wednesday. Oriana and I went for a run down by Westlake this afternoon. It was much colder, mid-40s. We decided, rather than stop and turn around at Diamond Marina and go back the way we came, as we usually do, to continue along Westlake to the intersection at Dexter and Nicholson, by the Fremont Bridge. We walked down a small road with virtually no traffic (one car went by) where there are rows of houseboats that extend all the way to the Aurora Bridge, which arched above us with its immense network of steel girders, reminding me a little of looking up at the network of steel girders on the Eiffel Tower. Oriana reminded me of a suicide that had recently occurred. A young woman had somehow managed to climb up the protective fencing along the bridge railing, and jump to her death. How strange that must be to live in such close proximity to such tragedy. Imagine, I said, having a suicide suddenly appear on your dining table.

It was the Day of the Dead. All Souls Day. The dark asphalt was constellated with huge yellowish leaves. The lassitude of late afternoon was filled with gleaming correspondences. Is there anything more radical than a shovel full of fungus? If I ever get a tattoo on my back it will be a canary or an armadillo. That's how I felt about the breeze at that moment. Sad as a banana.

I thought there was a flight of steps on the west side of the Fremont Bridge which would've allowed us to skip one of the lights of the intersection, but there wasn't. We had to wait for two lights. This intersection is insanely huge and complicated. Seattle is a city of intersections. It's also a city of improvisations, having to accommodate sudden growths in population, first due to gold, then Microsoft and the tsunami of electronics that followed. The lights are long. I could set up a folding chair and read Tolstoy's *War and Peace* while waiting for the light to change.

We walked up Fourth, which is astonishingly high and steep. Just walking up Fourth is like flying in an airplane. You go up so fast. It's fun. You can turn around and look all the way over to Phinney Ridge, where the Woodland Park Zoo resides, and the poet Philip Lamantia once lived, and could hear the lions roar in the morning. I mean Phinney Ridge the neighborhood, not the zoo. Philip did not live in the zoo. But he could hear the zoo. As I do now. In the still of a November night. Not a real zoo, no. A zoo of metaphors. And spider monkeys. And trumpeter swans doing Miles. And giraffes nibbling glissandos in the dampness of funny Phinney Ridge.

We walked down Bigelow and I thought of Kauai. Because I was cold (sweaty then still equals cold) and to imagine a warm tropical climate smeared my mind with glorious sunlight. The gossip of palm fronds in a tropical breeze.

Oriana reminds me each day how much time before we leave for Kauai. I've been trying to get in the mood for travel. Psyched, as they say. I'm not big on travel these days, maybe it's age, maybe it's the disintegration of everything, the ravages of pandemic and climate change catastrophe and war and neoliberal economics, the sadness, the despair and graffiti and prostitution. I try turning all that around like a lazy Susan to look at the benefits of travel. There are constants. Travel is stressful, but also stimulating, I mean hugely stimulating, everything is new, dislocated, you're outside time, outside your anesthetizing habits, the structure of events and people you've built around your life, the architecture of the everyday. You're displaced. Tired. Craving rest. Quiet. There's excitement as soon as you enter a lobby and go through the usual ritual. Get a key card, open the door, walk in, and the quiet embraces you, pulls you into its comfort zone. Flop on the bed. Ignore the luggage. Wallow in that interval between disarray and hurry and pandemonium. That's what I love about hotels: the voluptuousness of anonymity.

Take that Edward Hopper painting, for example, *Hotel Room*, with the woman sitting on the edge of a freshly made bed wearing nothing but a slip and holding a thick paperback on her lap; it's such a wonderful moment, so relaxed, her luggage still on the floor, unpacked, plenty of time to get to it later, but for now what's important, is this book, this riveting passage, this loaf of time. The writer said this is a painting of loneliness. No, it's not. Does this woman look lonely to you? Is this an American obsession, loneliness? Like there's something weird about being alone, or feeling comfortable in whatever solitude one can grab for oneself, and simplicity, the wonderful simplicity that comes with solitude, when the madhouse pandemonium of the social arena has been shoved sweetly aside and the time has come to focus, to let the senses dilate, and discover life.

Hotels are inherently literary. You sense it immediately as soon as you step into the lobby. If it's a big lobby, you're in a big production. Expect to see Fred Astaire tap dance toward your luggage. Mae West will hold the elevator door for you. If it's a small hotel, there'll be a little bell on the counter and a woman in a polka dot dress reading *Sense and Sensibility* on Kindle. Always, Ritz or Ramada, is a desk in the room. It's inviting in a strange way. It seems to be saying come here and write something. Something full of weltschmertz and charm. Insights are the flowers of inquiry. Regrets are the currency of the street. The coinage of alienation. And so I made my decision. I'm mailing myself to the Kuiper Asteroid Belt, c/o God, or anyone willing to take me. Dear Universe, I'm a refugee stuck at the border between grim acceptance and Edward Hopper, can you get me out of here, I'll do anything you ask (within reason).

A change of medium can be psychotropic. I recommend water ski-ing when it comes to anything boisterous and fun and maintaining balance. Parasailing whenever you feel cherubic like Reubens. And when it comes to the supramundane we have romance, knights with lances in good humor, exchanging jokes and making light of the situation, the dark ages and all of its underlying factors, such as the sheer irrationality of human behavior, and the need for armor. Dragons are a blessing. They bring a vivid energy to our discussions around the fire. So please. Enjoy the conjecture. Electrical current is a circular flow. The electric field that is applied to the wire causes the electrons that are inside the wire to move. This movement involves electrical resistance, which in turn causes heat, and the emission of photons, or *Huckleberry Finn*. You and a book under a lamp. You and a lamp and Vivaldi riding the canals of Venice with a violin.

I watch a YouTube video about Edward Hopper. I have a poet friend very much interested in Hopper and we exchanged some email concerning Hopper and the knee-jerk assumption of loneliness in his paintings. There's so much more than mere loneliness going on in his paintings. As for YouTube, it's become a major feature of my life. I listen to music almost constantly. When I saw the reference to Hopper in the YouTube feed, it was a little disquieting, a sure sign of surveillance. Most of the time, I'm amused by the choices the algorithms cough up, depending on the patterns of my listening history. Lots of classical (Bach, Mozart, Vivaldi) and lots of rock, The Kills, Mark Lanegan, Bob Dylan, Karen Carpenter. Yes, Karen Carpenter. That one surprised me. But her voice is sublime. Likewise Yvonne Elliman, Etta James and Aretha Franklin. And whenever the upstairs neighbors starts banging around in the kitchen I go in search of big sounds, full sounds, a density of music whose volumes and intricacies are oceanic.

I listen to music a lot, generally on earphones. It's become an environment, an immersion, like Jonah in the whale. In a real whale you'd be mucking about in krill and hydrochloric acid. But this is an allegorical whale. The immersion is biblical. It's in the belly of the whale that Jonah finds revelation, a dissolution of the ego that leads to a divine understanding. Immersion is conversion. Consciousness becomes cosmic. Oceanic. And when the whale vomits Jonah on a beach, he becomes a mighty surfer, and people come to listen to his story of immersion at night before a flaming bonfire, which I just now added, because I like bonfires, they remind me of good times, and because I'm a whale. The universe is a perpetual, protean swarming of things, a theater of ephemeral phenomena. We're processes. We're flux. And 180 tons of blubber.

Once I faced my agitation I felt better. I had my daily morning spoon, my evening repast, and my fiddle. Bliss was a bushy crust of moss. I found a good place to make my pants shake. I stood inside and shook with them. Pants are complex. I'm constantly trying to understand them. I wrote a report and then erased it. This is my life, my bounce, my spin, my toss of the ball. The ball hits the wall and bounces back and that's just fine, it's what I've come to expect of physical reality. What I was seeking was plasmatic and numinous and could only be found by unmuzzling the beast within and letting it exult in the oratory of the bloodmobile. Life was a continuous bombast. I found no maturity along the way, only swimming, which was a form of chronicle. Each stroke of my arms, each kick of my legs, brought me closer to significance. I wanted that quality of the deepened, the seasoned, and the wet. I climbed out of the pool and felt reborn. Water plays an important role in my life, a bit like Jean Simmons as Ophelia, thrashing about in a state of utter confusion. It didn't help that I lived by a lake of oddly contrived woodsheds. The respect for tools seemed somehow based in pharmaceuticals. I used various oils for wallowing in my memory. The day developed jelly. The night developed strands. When I closed my eyes, an ooze of biography collapsed into snow and jewelry. I don't understand myself. Nobody understands themselves. Sometimes I think I've got the script down pat and the scene changes and I'm lost once again. But that's another story. For which I'm eternally auditioning.

I like reading Ted Berrigan's prose, his memoirs and journals, chiefly from the 1970s, a decade I remember well. I'm fascinated by the way he deals with poverty. I almost said poetry. Poetry and poverty do tend to go together. Berrigan makes references to being broke, but does so in a neutral tone, there's no groaning, no acerbity thrown at fate or the full moon in the window of a railroad flat in lower Manhattan. He refers to poverty as a fact. A thing in the lives of poets that's bound to occur now and then, like a cold, or an allergy, depending on the frequency. I knew as soon as I committed to being a writer at age eighteen after a full immersion in *Les fleurs du mal* by Charles Baudelaire that poverty would be a fact of life. I didn't realize the full extent of it until I began experiencing it, and realizing that it changes according to age. Being poor in your twenties isn't that bad. It's easy if you're single. A little harder if you're married. Marriages tend not to do well in poverty, particularly if one member is a poet and the other tries holding down jobs and struggling to rise higher in the professional world. This is not a good formula. But if, like Ted and Alice Notley, both are poets, then it's far more tolerable within the dynamics of a marriage. Berrigan doesn't allude to poverty as a kind of martyrdom, though it's easy to sense the rapport he felt with Japanese poet Bashō, and the simpleness by which he lived. It wasn't stoical. It had a natural feel to it. Ted liked drugs, too. That's going to complicate things. But he seemed to glide through these obstacles like some guy in a kayak going down the Colorado River. No complication got too complicated. Berrigan doesn't appear to have gotten into heroin or cocaine. That's a prescription for disaster. Mostly pot, amphetamine and booze. Good combo for writers. You can sit in front of a typewriter and feel the flow glow through your fingers to the keys and get splattered like agates against the platen, waves of perturbation smashing against the walls.

Heavy winds last night. The streets were full of leaves that had the transparency and liquid glow of life. But were dead. Quite dead. So dead they seemed alive. Like the way brooks and streams will sometimes approximate the sensual fullness of a satisfied need yet never completely pinch the right frets, being of another world. The water glistens because it's water, and because it's water, it smashes hard and cold against the skin. Water is vital to earth, there's nothing earthier than water when you're thirsty or lounging in a hot tub on the slope of an alpine mountain, but it's also transparently otherworldly. It evaporates and becomes clouds. Rain and lightning and heavy winds. Or a violinist opening her eyes to make sure she's still standing on a floor.

The gypsy woman had a large red lampshade in her caravan tasseled with snowballs. She peered into her globe and whatever she saw filled with her eyes with terror and amazement. What is it? I asked. She shook her head. I cannot say, she said. But if your neighborhood should fill with rabbits, look to it my friend, for these are omens. Omens, gnomons. Once you begin looking for omens you begin seeing omens everywhere. Sidewalks go gothic and twirl around in chalk. Hilary Hahn plays her violin until it lights on fire. A ghost sits in our bathtub every night playing with a pair of pliers. I think it's John Lennon. The fabric separating the real from the unreal is very thin. A lot of stuff gets through. Electromagnetism, sunflowers, and coral. Last night I saw Bob Dylan playing pool with Marlene Dietrich. And the neighborhood is teeming with rabbits.

We don't know where they came from, all these rabbits. We see them in the park, in people's driveways and gardens, running from shrub to shrub. It's spooky. Sometimes we'll see one dead on the sidewalk with its head ripped off. There's also a surprising number of owls new to the neighborhood.

We return from a run, shower, get dressed and go on an errand for a tuna and pumpkin cat food Molly loves. It's 3:00 in the afternoon but dark as night due to the thickness of the clouds. It's raining with the force of a monsoon. I've got the wipers going full blast, whick-a-whack whick-a-whack whick-a-whack, I can barely see, and the traffic is heavy. And brutal. Seattle drivers don't have road rage: they embody road rage. Their frustrations with family and work, with the cold indifference of the universe, get played out behind the wheel. Even on a calm day they look ahead with visceral intent: get out of my way. You definitely don't want to encounter these people in the early morning on their way to work. The bus is a much better choice. Who doesn't love the anonymity of the bus? The delicious loss of control and absence of responsibility. But here I am behind the wheel, anxious, alert, contemptuous of the other drivers.

I park the car and Oriana gets out to get the cat food. I'd go with her, but the warmth in the car feels so good I don't want to get out. Soon after she leaves the warmth dissipates quickly and I begin getting cold and regret not going with her. I would've enjoyed seeing the birds. Oriana returns with the cat food and we circle around the hill to go to the pot shop for some cannabis gummies. Just as the left turn light turns green and I enter the intersection, we hear the loud honking of a fire engine and I panic not knowing where it's coming from and stop behind the other car and the big red engine races by and disappears back into the rain.

We have dinner (Greek pasta) and watch another episode of *Extraordinary Attorney Woo.*

8:36 P.M. I sit down at my desk with a bottle of water, a bottle of antacid lozenges, and interview Tristan Tzara:

Q: Do you like to make your bed in the morning?

A: Absolutely. I use a sledgehammer. I get insights by reaching for the pillows. I keep a trapeze under a stuffed horse. I use it to swing back and forth like a trombone stuck in a jujube.

Q: What do you think of today's propaganda?

A: I think it's terrific. I've never seen so many brainwashed people. I mean, what an achievement! We've finally reached a point where someone with a different viewpoint is persecuted like Joan of Arc. No society can function like this. Therefore, propaganda should be the national religion. All it requires is a ruthless disregard for truth. Propaganda is a virus that will bring the so-called civilized world down. Our species will be erased. The world will become pristine again. We are a failed species, but we did help bring newspeak and agitprop into being, which proved to be the DNA of our undoing. Propaganda is the wicked genius of fiction. It is to be regarded with great respect, and the flourish of a hand in a white parade glove.

Q: Have you ever worked in a mine?

A: Do you mean mine, or mind? I've worked in a number of mines, and minds. I discovered a vein of gold in a bus driver once. He was totally incompetent. He kept driving the bus over the sidewalk. I descended into his mind and discovered his whole secret depended on pessimism.

Q: How do you feel about the American embassy in Morocco?

A: It's a crumpling temperament, a fragile disaster of soap. I can taste the apricot in the mouth of the traveler at the end of a long day exploring the streets of Tangiers. I see William S. Burroughs seated behind the desk, fanning himself with a multicolored bamboo fan and offering a lump of hashish on a silver platter to his guests and applicants. I offer a salute. And thank him for his service.

Q: What are your feelings about music?

A: They're mostly red, the kind of red you see at Christmas, or on the nose of an alcoholic butcher with a passion for Bach. When I listen to Karen Carpenter I want to run around the house naked trailing a bright red scarf. Jimi Hendrix makes me foggy, like tomorrow's pants, red of course, with hundreds of pockets and a parachute. John Cage opens my mind. J. J. Cale blows my mind. Keith Richards conducts mass with a boogie piano and a bell tower of chapped percussion.

Q: How do you feel about Jerry Lee Lewis?

A: I become incandescent and masturbate.

Q: Do you understand electricity?

A: I don't, no. I think it's got something to do with electrons or something. Is it onions? It's a dramatic medium, isn't it? It's not exactly Dada. It's so purposeful. All those wires leading up to something. Toasters, tortillas, and tacit assumptions. Have you ever been shocked? The muscles ripple with its energy. I don't know. Maybe the secret of electricity is Dada. Electricity is the mother of Dada.

Q: What do you think Heidegger meant by "Transcendence constitutes selfhood"?

A: I haven't the faintest idea. Let me ask you something: what are you doing this for?

Q: Doing what?

A: Interviewing a dead man you've never met and trying to pass it off as some sort of journalistic éclat or literary feat. Don't you think that's a little pretentious, not to mention dishonest?

Q: Ok, you got me. I've been exposed. But isn't this fun?

A: It's fun. Yes. I'd like to go back to being dead now if you don't mind.

Q: Sure thing. Thank you for your patience.

A: Hi-ho, Silver! And away!

Tuesday morning is rough. Just at the moment consciousness begins seeping into my brain and I look forward to those
voluptuous moments lingering in bed for a few more minutes
while I get used to the whole idea of being alive and aware and
marooned on planet Earth in the body of a seventy-five-year-
old man, our upstairs neighbor fired up his dishwasher. It's not
a quiet dishwasher. It sounds like the engine of a Douglas DC
8. Why this fool is running a dishwasher at all is perplexing. He
lives alone. He spends hours in the kitchen. Even so: how many
plates and forks does a single guy need? He seems devoted to
food. He's not fat. His devotion to food is labor-intensive and
requires a lot of attention. Eating is a discipline. This isn't com-
pulsive eating this is athletic eating. It's a challenge. It's Spartan,
not a luxury. I hear exigency in the noises. The crashes and bangs
and endless chopping. I'm sure he's not conscious of making all
that racket or going about things with such aggression. It passes through the floor like the toxic undercurrents of a business
office, the unspoken resentments, the moments of panic, the
afflicting frustrations. You can feel it. The tightness. Your entire
body becomes a fist. It's a poor way to start a day.

I've never been a particularly humble person. My cynicism goes
too deep. I don't expect anything from anybody except aque-
ducts, highways, and embroidery. I'm not sure this is the correct
place for humility. Humility likes a habitat full of flapjacks and
quiet early morning jokes. Innocuous observations. Benedictions
of butter. Slippery Joe and his magic duodenum. Human society
was too much for me. I longed for reality and paper. I joined the
secret societies of the grey and sporadic. I gleaned admonitions
from the border between engagement and exultation and came
away feeling raw as a headlight. I dyed my hair the color of out-
rage. I twisted my arms into flowers. Elves winked at my plum-

age. I asked God for more time and was given a diving board and a helicopter. I rubbed a Sunday afternoon into a vertebral understanding of sequence. On another occasion, I swooned like a rock in a drama of adjectives and beans. And when it all came crashing down I fought my way out of bed and got dressed and made breakfast. I got dressed in a fish and went to work doing nothing. It's what I'm good at. It's what I do when there's nothing else to do. I circle the aquarium endlessly, postulating my movement with fins.

It excites me to think of the Queen of England kicking a soccer ball. Not the late Elizabeth II, but Elizabeth I, the one that delivered a moving speech at Tilbury before the English fleet went to meet the Spanish Armada, presided over a flourishing economy and enjoyed performances of Shakespeare. I picture her in one of those huge gowns kicking the ball. I see the gown swinging back and forth with little gold and silver brocade threads catching the light of the sun. It's a gratuitous image, of no importance to anyone, and cumbersomely anachronistic. Hardly worth the effort to write down. But this is the problem with words. They must be directed toward some purpose, carpentry or spectacle, or they atrophy and drop from the brain like overripe fruit, perfuming the air with fermentation. I like the way that guy Hamlet used them, embroidering the air with contemplations of suicide, joking with gravediggers, and conversing with ghosts. Be thou assured, if words be made of breath, and breath of life, they must be worth something, even if it's just to say nothing, and do nothing, and churn out diatribes on the turpitudes of existence.

One day Henry Miller floated by on a surfboard with a toothpick and a wry smile and said nobody should stagger through the world needing things. I agree. The world is based on a palimpsest of assumptions. A word is a worm with a genius for burrowing into the brain and loosening the soil and making it fertile for the production of beans and philosophy. Things like frost, sprockets, watermarks, and the drool of a dazzling mist as it brushes over the cypress on the high cliffs of Big Sur. At the end of the day what counts is that feeling you get at the bottom of a swimming pool that you're very near to entering another dimension. And that becomes poetry and the poetry becomes an addiction to the hypothetical, a fondness for the lopsidedness of drunken lobsters, and the expression on a waitress's face receiving an order for eggs benedict.

I like to translate things. Long lonesome nights in Kansas. The sociability of spoons, the dare of paradise and the knee of a caribou. All sorts of enigmas await the embouchure of a tongue, the bruise of a breathless vowel, and a compound predicate lying on a cloud of pastry flour. Hell is just a prank. It is untranslatable into any language. If you're looking for comfort, English has power steering and advanced navigation. But if you're looking for the adventure of a lifetime in quantum mechanics and enjoy the desert and the psychotropic venom of toads, I recommend Hopi. French is wonderful for food. German has power and philosophy. Ibo is nimble and polyvalent. I can't speak for fog. I don't understand what it's trying to say. Same with water. One day it's clouds, the next day it's rain. One day it's a shower, the next day snow. What kind of language is this? What is the muttering of a hyacinth? What is the true eloquence of moss? Is DNA a language? If DNA is a language, am I a grammar of carbon and nucleic acids? I like to think of myself as a Rosetta stone for the hieroglyphics on the back of a spiny orb-weaver.

I heard a man on BBC the other night who talked about the incredible distance spiders are able to fly. It spews a strand of silk, spun into fiber by the spinnerets on the spider's belly, lets the breeze catch it and, voila!, the spider is airborne.

I don't oppose the ooze of a rawhide collar stud, nor do I spurn the flutter of a proposal if it drops to the floor in a sudden apoplexy of incompatible subjectivity. I see a stirring beam amid the gossip that the algebra of the socially maladroit expands into a canoe. Therefore, it behooves me to redeem the time with a little transcendence. Let's get spectral. I'll hymn an itch we can texture. If you play with experience, an absence with meat on its bones will grab you and burn you. Afterwards, an eager reflection will climb on your back during your metamorphosis and make you circumspect. I'll fire up the forge and make a padlock. The fly the dissolve the alpaca. Everything I shape shouts tulip. Tumult is a cartoon your string has caused to thrive. I think you have a beautiful throat. You look good with a wild skull and a clean curl.

Icelandic Viking poet Egil Skallagrímsson — who composed his first poem at age three and grew to be a fierce berserker — had Paget's disease, which causes a deformation of bone, and is speculated to be the cause of Egil's large and unattractive head. Or maybe it was because it contained so much poetry.

Sometimes it feels good to put your foot on the floor and get up slowly and reenter the world stage. There's no script, but you don't have to memorize any lines. It's all improv. What comes out of you may have something to do with the people you encounter. Or the other actors on the world stage. The incomprehensible depravity and predatory greed of the elites at the expense of the working class, now invisible, mopping floors, driving people to the airport, cutting hair, flipping burgers, repairing pipes, erecting steel beams, wracked with worry, but with both feet on the ground. And sometimes in the darkness the true mystery of the universe seeps in and leaves a little light for the next morning, the next demand, the next corner, the next nexus, the next exit.

Beauty slides its sugar into the unknown excursion some consider worth a few candles and a little money. Too many thorns in the kitchen will spoil the poultry. Distance is such a mournful thing. Few consider it comprehensible. Last night a memory blew through my mind and left a kettle on the ceiling. There's a reason for everything. Except regret. No enigma is hollow. The very effort to solve it gives it a meaning and an interior celebrity. François Hardy or Charles Bronson. An unresolved problem will swell into a mailbox and fill with letters from all thirteen colonies of my tablecloth. The man with a mended eye is the one to see what's wrong and so misunderstood about understanding. And I stood there blinking at the brightness of the foundry.

I'm feeling bullish and so hum a yellow song. It was written by a sewer rat in Paris who knew Victor Hugo personally. It's a beautiful song, and yellow as the advocacy at the core of the sun. Humming helps me understand the parsley family. No foam or agitation of the sea has as much sheer aggression as the carrot. Can you smell it? There's a bear in the oyster farm. I love ovals. And cubes and cones and cylinders. Cylinders especially. These are some of the shapes I've learned while making guitars for The Rolling Stones. I study closely how women apply lipstick with careful loving strokes, and then imitate it when I'm playing hockey. I can't, for the life of me, understand how anyone could put their trust in a government. Life is an equation served cold. It takes more than calipers to anatomize its features. The laws are created to protect money. I didn't discover ethics until I discovered flight. I joined the Chippewa of the Turtle Mountains and kneeled in the mud of the Missouri getting a drink. That's what I mean by fulfillment.

Oriana arrives home from Fred Myer and tells me they didn't have a door rack. They carry them, but they were sold out. I need a new door rack because the current one — chrome — rusted, weirdly. I didn't think chrome could rust. Apparently, it can. My white running socks started getting speckles on them from the rusted hooks. She also saw Bob Dylan's new book *The Philosophy of Modern Music*. We decided to go back and get it. I was intrigued with the people on the cover. Little Richard, Eddie Cochran and a short young individual sandwiched between them with impeccably groomed blonde hair, the bangs combed up in a jump of exuberance, an attractive face with a facile lipstick smile, wearing a corduroy jacket and holding an acoustic guitar with a patch above the bridge where the varnish had worn away by the hand going up and down doing chords. I couldn't tell if it was a man or a woman. I guessed woman. Who was this person? We found it was a young woman named Alis Lesley, touted as the female Elvis Presley. She started out like gangbusters, doing rockabilly tunes and soulful love ballads, then suddenly disappeared. Quite a mystery. There's always an enigma touching on anything Bob Dylan does.

I like this book. I like the writing and the whole idea of a song being a world, a stance, a philosophy. Even a nutty tune like "Tutti Frutti" can hit you like a wild balmy spring and a-wop-bop-a-loo-bop a-wop-bam-boom. The philosophy here is obvious: glossolalia puts the gloss on Hegel's phenomenality of spirit. Dylan's selections are often as obscure as they are enlightening.

"The 'Phenomenology' is thus a sort of freely told philosophy of history. It begins with the Spirit on a crude and sensual stage;

it follows his paradoxes, his social enlargement, his perplexities, his rebellions, his skepticism, all his wanderings, until he learns, through toils and anguish and courage, such as represent the whole travail of humanity, that he is, after all, in his very essence the absolute and divine spirit himself, who is present already on the savage stage in the very brutalities of master and slave; who comes to a higher life in the family; who seeks freedom again and again in romantic sentimentality or in stoical independence, who learns, however, always afresh that in such freedom there is no truth; who returns, therefore, willingly to the bondage of good citizenship and of social morality; and who, finally, in the religious consciousness, comes to an appreciation of the lesson that he has learned through this whole self-enlarging process of civilization — the lesson, namely, that all consciousness is a manifestation of the one law of spiritual life, and so, finally, of the one Eternal Spirit."

—Josiah Royce, *The Spirit of Modern Philosophy* 215–16

Little Richard could've written that. He sang it instead. It's got "Tutti Frutti" all over it.

There are songs I can listen to repeatedly without getting tired of them. "The Song of the Muddy Banana in the Dirty Bandana" performed by Steady State Slim and the Merry Variables is one. It helps me achieve the somnolence of stone, and the celestial wisdom of elephants in the forests of Ghana. I remember my nervousness around guns. We pay a heavy price for subtlety. Each word is a nail. Each kitchen drawer a monad. The sound it makes when I open it is a brightness felicitous as a glowworm. I call it "The Song of the Siren Knives." Though it's mostly about forks, with an epilogue of spoons. Sometimes I can hear the fruit rotting on the ground and it makes me want to dance a bunch of words into a paragraph where there's a chance to be reborn as a temperament or a corkscrew. It ends with a mournful cream, and a referendum of intimacy.

There are songs that bring back moments, vivid moments, occasions of depth and intensity. A song that happened to be playing during a moment of sudden insight can root itself so deeply in your being that every time you hear it that emotion and its occasion returns with a serendipitous lucidity. All the sensations return. Chronological time is replaced by a long horizon. You think it's there, but as you move toward it, it recedes. Its existence feeds on the energy you've derived from its being. It's a circular give and take. Like an ouroboros. Ra and Osiris in the underworld.

Given a choice between being hunted or haunted I would choose haunted. I can do haunted anywhere, on a bus, in bed, at the breakfast table, at a podium during a conference with the darkness looming behind me, collecting rocks in the desert, or ordering a steak dinner at a candlelight dinner in Saint Louis, Missouri. Hunted is terrible. Someone, some thing out there, wants you dead. Or found. And not found for any good reason. Every moment is tense when you're hunted. Your senses are on the alert. Being haunted is similar. The difference is in the dimensionality of the situation. There are two dynamics involved. Hunting occurs on the outside. Haunting occurs on the inside. You can hide from whoever or whatever is hunting you. But you can't hide from what's haunting you. You can try to drown it with a fifth of tequila. But ghosts don't drown. You have to purge them. Atone, forgive, redeem, absolve, exonerate oneself. This may take a little religion. A little sacrifice maybe. Prayer and incantation. A pilgrimage to the Amazonian basin. Ayahuasca or psilocybin. And the right spirit. Which must be hunted.

I've got all my hygiene particulars ready for our trip to Kau-ai. Shaving lather, disposable razors, mouthwash, galvanometer, evangelical crystals, a typewriter ribbon from the Ming Dynasty for wrapping around my head at night, and a box of antonyms for when I'm feeling disagreeable. I'm lacking a comb. I'm not bringing my brush, it's too big, and too cumbersome. Hair gets caught among the bristles. It's like a columbarium of hair. A comb is adequate for what used to be a forest of hair. The forest is gone. In its place is a genteel layering of filamentary beach grass. It can easily be tamed with a few gentle strokes of a modest but adequate comb. I'll also need a sandwich bag for my pharmaceuticals, and a headphone cord. This is who I am. What I am. What I'm all about. Geriatrics, hygiene, and occasional dereliction. Estrangement, repudiation, nonfeasance. Some apostasy. Some lapses. Some minor rebellions against the prevailing order.

Oriana wants me to wear a mask on the plane. She believes that masks protect you from Covid. I do not. Wearing a mask is humiliating. It makes me feel silly. But if I were to get Covid (and getting Covid is a real possibility, mask or no mask), I would be left in Kauai feeling foolish, self-centered, and repen-tant. Not to mention worried about how to get home. Or spend the night.

Ironic, that one must endure so much humiliation to ascend to 30,000 feet in the air.

My nose started to bleed today. Fortunately, I was in the bath-room. Each time a drop of blood hit the tile I was able to wipe it up with a paper towel. It was a little hard coordinating the blood dropping while wiping it up, but once I managed to stop the bleeding with a small wad of paper towel in my nose, I could give my full attention to wiping blood up from the floor and sink. Don't know what got it going. The air is pretty dry today. The veins grew brittle. Maybe that's it. My sinuses have been weird lately. I need to calm everything down with a little Mersey sound. "Everyone's Gone to the Moon" sung by Jonathan King. So loaded with nostalgia I can grow a big antenna on Sunday and catch Wolfman Jack. Songs like trinkets on the rump of rebellion. The embarrassment of revealing a feeling. A shirk in a hurt shirt. Everyone's gone to the moon.

Suddenly there's a shift in perception. Something's different. It's very subtle. But you can feel it in the room. Napoleon doing a handstand, ions making a proton parade, rupees dancing in a meadow of antifreeze. A dead metronome on the periphery of the known world. A dead rhythm with a down-turned bill and a rebounding skyscraper hat is opening a lid of candor on a patio obloquy. I can sense it. I know it's there. And there it is. I left the pharmacy lamp on.

The indefinability of Being wiggles a finger in the slippery core of the universe and creates a catalogue of carpet selections and pile options. Can there be a softness so soft it's hard? Being is soft. And hard. Existence isn't easy. It takes a lot of hammering and yelling and carefully worded contracts. This is why people sit in their parked cars gazing at warranties. You know what I mean. Everything you need to know in life is bulbous. The mind is hungry. What's going on in your head this minute? Never mind. It's a very personal question. We should keep things on a formal basis until we get to know one another better. I don't remember much of my arrival. I was probably wet, and crying. And here I am many years later, gazing at a print: *The Origin of the World*, by Gustave Courbet. If you aren't familiar with it, that's fine. We've all been there.

Which do you prefer, transparence or translucence? Do you like seeing things clearly, or a little vague, a little blurry? I like them a little blurred. I prefer metaphors and bizarre conceits to the literal and well-defined. Oranges to apples. Stories to manuals. Wild animals to zoos. Snoozing to oozing. Enzymes to dimes. Coffeehouses to schools. Puns to guns. Sideshows to circuses. Paper towels to napkins. Notepaper to newspaper. Beckett to bucket. Bucket to Beckett. Woolf to Wolf. I'm beginning to veer. Beginning to stray. I prefer it. Prefer meanders to straight shots. Backroads to freeways. Detours to direct routes. Fucking off to pursuing a career. Jalopies to Teslas. Phantasmagoric to pyrophoric. Beginning a subject then losing focus and finding yourself playing roulette with bitcoins in Monaco after a long and protracted fugue state.

If you want to begin, you should begin at the beginning but not always. Spit. Swear. Jump in the pool. Make a splash. You can't always generate sticky substances in a confused mass and expect this to be poetry. But sometimes you can. You'll see mouths full of chocolate, drooling, and believe this is the *quattrocento* all over again. Take endurance. Take it outside and beat it up. Keep at it. If it resists, persist. When you're finished, come back inside and we'll rip the air with our voices and cause lima beans to explode into bistros and chiaroscuro to make significant contributions to the world of the loon. This is a dream, isn't it? Now we're getting somewhere. I'm in my favorite room. The one with the chandelier draped with live rattlesnakes. Think of a lake from your childhood. Sit down and poke it. See the ripples? Those are the years of your life. When they reach the shore, the ripples will have enlarged. We will begin to understand the chaos of the street. I've come a long way. I require some tranquility now. And a jackknife and a song.

This thing I invested my life in, poetry, feels strange to me in the current environment. This is not an era for poetry and art. Art has been coopted by the Woke crowd. It's all about diversity and identity politics. Art is an afterthought. The same trends have infected the poetry world, but there remain vectors of free speech and fertile grounds for the little black seeds we call words.

Poetry isn't a controlled substance, it's more like Indonesia. We have agates and gypsum and bicker like little Frisian bakers. We feel wisdom but conceal it with our iconoclasm. We get thinking on our friends and poetry on our clothes. We have cravings and enthusiasms. We need a motel room. One full of rotating ghosts and Florentine drapes. The small slow smolder of old emotional debts. The smell of poetry which is fragrant in the eyes of the Queens of Sonnetstan. We undertake a craze for beauty and whatever we happen to see becomes a windshield. Or a habitat for hiking and centaurs. We feel effulgent and annoy the tarpaulin with our sympathy. It's a tarpaulin, after all, not a shawl for the winds of midnight. There's always a little boat involved. The poetry happens when the oars appear stroke forward then back and, voila!, we're moving.

The Tree of Heaven in the Stadtpark in Neunkirchen, Saarland, Germany, has a girth of almost five feet. I only bring it up because there's someone standing on my feet and that someone is me. Which is a lie because I'm lying. I'm a cavern-dwelling creature. I'm a spelunker, I'm a bat. Expect nothing from me except darkness. A ten pound bag of potatoes and a ticket to paradise. That is if you're willing to sign a waiver. I can't promise you paradise will be safe or even be paradise. I can, however, promise you a rose garden. These will be imaginary roses, of course, in an imaginary garden in a completely real sentence hovering over a sheet of paper in a state of considerable potential, not to mention tension, and a little tergiversation. I apologize for the cheese. It was meant to be Roquefort and came up chedder. Sang the Spirits of Gouda.

I've got to be careful with the water bottle they made the caps smaller. I have to fumble with it to get it on right. I'm not an astronaut. But I could be, given a sufficient amount of space, a drop of beatitude, and a lot of altitude. I float in the void twisting a bolt while planet earth glows blue and white below me. Problems are always so public. They feel private but really they're not. They're smoky and interwoven. As much fabric as fabrication. And when they go away they collapse into gratitude. So they're still there. Still issues. Matter at hand. But you can sit on them. It's best to keep on the bright side when the plant shuts down. When the world goes topsy-turvy. And your pants don't fit. This is how the stegosaurus became gasoline. And horses horsepower.

Last night I woke up in the middle of the Jurassic. I felt mint, and offhand, and highly elastic. I was able to reason by using an alias. And a good alibi. Logic never came easy to me. It made too much sense. It calibrated things equally and caused symmetry and balance. I looked for substitutes in filigree and garage bands. This is when gravity appeared and I became weightless as a result of being too new to gravity to believe it. The more I understood, the more convinced I became the heavier I became until at last I had to sit down. But the legs of the chair were pointing up at the sky and my head was looking down at the ground. I could see texture, and pyramids, and piranha. I could see minced garlic cloves and multilayeredness. This is known as the Paradox of Lasagna. It's nice to smell when it's coming, but bad to smell when it's gone.

I need some cataplasm for my ectoplasm. I need a star and a throat and a penumbral thong. One day I shall be president of a stroll. I wander through time like a biography with leavening other than yeast. I think history is a cash register. And a syllable is drinkable. The show is about to start. It may have already started. The grid is grinding itself in lamentation. I poured a bottle of prose all over a poem and it became a guitar. I can't make sense of anything. Except ocher.

8:00 P.M. Thursday. We walked down to Pike Place Market this afternoon. I was hoping to find a T-shirt for our upcoming trip to Kauai, something quirky, something droll, maybe a little edgy, but not too edgy. Airports have become very tense places. I don't know why any of this was important to me. But I thought it could use a little indulgence, if anything just to see where it took me. I remembered a stand at Pike Place Market that had a lot of nutty T-shirts and so that's where we headed. It was surprisingly balmy for a day in mid-November, about 52 degrees. But the real surprise was seeing how clean the streets were, free of the homeless encampments and people maneuvering drearily in austere and merciless conditions as we've become accustomed to seeing elsewhere in the city. The new mayor must've taken some drastic action. The equation remains unsettling, because you know the homeless populations have not suddenly been given homes; they must be somewhere, they're just not downtown in the more touristy areas.

I often wonder how many people leave the office fuming over an injustice or insult at work and already have the dialogue in progress for the next day discussion with their boss, and as soon as they begin seeing all the encampments of the homeless in parks and under bridges and compiled precariously on sidewalks they decide to be stoical and return to work with a renewed attitude.

: 111 :

The boss is an asshole. But maybe you can let this one slide. Keep quiet, keep cool, and keep your job.

We walked along the waterfront which was quite pleasant. The dock where Oriana's mother had seen Tom Jones perform was being eaten by a giant mechanical monster. More than half of the dock had been torn down. Piles of it were lying on a barge. The air was scented with creosote. There was also an enormous construction site in progress at what used to be the back steps leading up to Pike Place Market. A flag lady directed us, politely and amiably, to a detour.

We entered the grand old market and found it crowded as always. The crowds here are always happy. Buoyant. Even in the winter. Pike Place has a very strange effect on people. It's funky. As anomalous and strong-smelling as can be, from the omnipresent smell of fish to the occasional whiff of cinnamon bark or piroshki or tenzig momo patchouli. I felt I'd entered a time warp. A pre-pandemic, pre-inflationary, pre-technocratic, pre-dystopic, pre-ecoanxiety time warp.

We paused at a table of notebooks bound in leather. They felt soft to the touch. I didn't open any up so I don't know what the paper felt like. They were too expensive for the scribbling I'd planned on doing during our trip. I wanted something that would fit snugly in the breast pocket of my shirt. I found a pretty one with crows on it at one of many little tchotchke shops. Only later did I realize T-shirts don't generally have breast pockets. Breast pockets on shirts seem to have gone the way of bookstores, libraries, free speech and literacy.

The T-shirts on display at the stand I was looking for were all a bit too provocative for a day at the airport. One said, "CNN

Sucks," another "I'm Not as Think as You Drunk I Am." One featured a multi-colored psychedelic skull and another featured a bosomy woman sitting on her heels in a wet shirt. I could just imagine the looks I'd get boarding a plane. Assuming they'd let me board the plane.

We continued our meander and I spotted a black T-shirt with a picture in white of an octopus curling its tentacles around the helmet of a deep-sea diver. The legend on it said "There's a Monster in the Water." It looked suitably comical and fun without being potentially incendiary, so I bought it for twenty-five bucks. I chose medium. I tried it on at home and it fit perfectly, but at 100% cotton, I'll have to make sure it doesn't go into the dryer after I wash it, or the diver will shrivel into moon jelly and the octopus will become an actuary.

Meanwhile, on the dentistry front, things are looking toothless. The woman who handles the insurance doesn't know how to handle my new Medicare plan which involves a reimbursement from the insurance company. They don't pay directly. She says I have to find the address and mail it in with the dental receipt. That doesn't sound right. I need to find a new dentist.

When things go wrong, I get granulated. I go all dark and mashed potatoes. *The New Yorker* is more enjoyable. Especially in a brown leather club chair. With a martini and a sandwich at my side. Olives are beautiful ontologies of themselves. If you close your eyes, you can see the universe dribbling a galaxy across the diaphragm of Belgium. Nothing here is real. It's been a macabre monotone all along the frequency for the entire bulging day. And by God I'm going to make some music out of it. I'll shuffle all the traffic lights until my insistence on Archimedean screws becomes appropriately helical. This is called Groovin'.

Felix Cavaliere in 2011 singing at the Pine Knob Music Theater. He looks old, but his voice is still young. He segues into The Temptations' "My Girl" and leans forward to get the notes just right. "I've got sunshine on a cloudy day. / When it's cold outside, I've got the month of May. / Groovin'. On a Sunday afternoon."

Where have all the beatniks gone? I never did like the hippies that much. I preferred the Beats. The hippies were goofy and affable but a bit vapid and a tad Pecksniffian. The Beats could be righteously grumpy. They weren't afraid of despair and leaning over the abyss to get a quick look at reality. They liked dark smoky bars and avant-garde jazz and maintaining a hardline against Babbitry. I prefer rock to jazz but what the hell. These aren't anthropological classifications. They're peregrinations. Concatenations. Will it come again? That paroxysm of creativity? Those existential haunts and weltschmerz? I'm getting mystical now. I'm absorbed. Neck deep in words. I'm bending over to pick up a sock. I'm laughing. Life is funny. One day you're a baby, the next you're a CFO in electrotherapy. You get lost in the world. You lose yourself. You find yourself. And this recurs. Quite frequently. And there you are. Sitting. Gazing into the air.

I have all the hardware I need to start a bohemian existence. Margo Timmins singing "Sweet Jane." Frank Zappa singing "You Are What You Is." I've got lanterns and pliers and tall white candles and sandpaper and eight pounds of sugar. I've got drugs and spells and incantations. I've got chronicles to share and energy to burn. I can glow in the dark and flame like a flamingo in the afternoon. I've got a brash rash and a kitchen sink. I've got all the right attitudes and a few wrong ones too. I don't wear mink, but I do feel effective around nudity. Hoes are my favorite gardening tool. But forget hoes. The best way to work the dirt is to use your hands. Never take a knife for granted. Avoid spending too much time in the toolshed. Go out and have some fun. Don't do anything I wouldn't do. I don't know what that means. But do it. No sleep is a slap in the Cubist bucket. What it is is unintentional. I agree. The string pulling this along is taut with song. And is so happy it's gleaming. Shining like a tint of nail polish on a thumb of punctuation.

The vertebral key is withered. Roast Island is in a storm. What are we going to do about the icing? What about the Northern Lights? What about pottery and skepticism? Let's resume size. Let's gerrymander a megabyte and send it home to West Hysteria. I'm a major general a polecat a rhythm and a honeycomb. Honey come comb my home. Shake your hips baby. It's easy. All you've got to do is stand there wiggling like a vast subjectivity in an unlicensed emergency.

Speaking frankly is again a pedagogical concern. For example, if I insert myself into your rheumatism, will I walk away with a free sample of you? A philosophical education can't be content with the study of texts chewed and rechewed until an acute thirst sets in. We need conceptions whose flexibility can be adapted to almost any situation that may arise on the fulfillment floor or dentist's office. We all bring something unique to the table. I'm an emissary of bliss and blister. Albeit more blister than bliss. So tell me: is life a prison? Do those shadows on the wall indicate a higher, truer reality awaiting us at the mouth of the cave? In reality, we grant that virtue produces a certain result, but we declare that what approximates to virtue, that is to say, progress, gives us technicolor. Logos spermatikos on the silver screen. Horse sense and saloons. Stoicism and saguaro. John Wayne carrying his saddle across the Arizona desert.

My desk is a small oak cabinet with a flap that comes down to provide a writing surface. It belonged to my grandmother in North Dakota, who kept a diary on it, quantity of cows milked, weather, things like that. I use it for writing nutty Dadaesque escapades in the English language, with occasional dalliances in French, which any French person would look upon with horror and call linguistic torture were they to see it. I'm surprised I wasn't jailed for breaking the French language when I was last in France for my halting, brutal and awkward attempts at speaking it. As for the flap, there are two metal strips joined together that bend like an elbow on one side and a brass chain on the other. The screw fastening the upper metal strip where it pivots had come loose. The hole had eroded. A little sawdust sprinkled down when I pulled the screw out. It was a binding head machine screw, blunt on the pointy end. I don't know why a machine screw rather than a wood screw had been used. It was also newer than the other screws, which dated back to the 1920s. Had I put it there? I had no memory of it. Not surprising. I have little memory of anything recent. But the horrors of my past, oh my yes, my brain is full of its colorful pageantry.

Driving anywhere in Seattle is stressful. Our neighborhood — which sits atop a hill and encompasses approximately three square miles — is no exception. To call it overcrowded is an understatement. It teems with people, most of them wealthy, and driving luxury cars, Tesla, Lexus and Mercedes Benz. You don't want to hit a Tesla, Lexus or Mercedes Benz. I came close once, while I was parallel parking. The rear view mirror in our Subaru makes it hard to gauge distance; objects appear closer than they actually are. So I moved back with extreme slowness. I felt a slight resistance and stopped. I barely touched the Tesla behind me, but the woman was already out of her car taking a picture of her front end with her smartphone. I filled with fear and rage. I got out. She was already back in her car. Wise move, lady. Her window was up, so I yelled "I didn't hit your car." "Yes, you did," she yelled back. There was no damage. Not a scratch. I walked away fuming. Have I yet mentioned how much I despise rich people?

I made a right turn on Queen Anne Avenue, right by the veterinarian clinic where we take Molly — and encountered a fire engine stopped in the lane, red lights blinking and whirling. The Presbyterian church cafeteria appeared to be on fire. The man in front of me decided he wasn't going to wait and backed up. I couldn't move back, there was a car behind me. He came close but didn't hit me. When he stopped, off to our immediate right, I gestured that I had nowhere to go. Whatever his next maneuver entailed, I was unable to participate in his choreography. Fortunately, the left lane was clear so we got around the fire engine and continued on our way. I parked a few cars up from the hardware store and opened my door just as a bicyclist whizzed past, veering slightly to avoid collision, and scaring the hell out of me.

The hardware store (they always smell so good) had an impressive array of machine screws, all the drawers full and clearly marked. The wood screws were in a small cabinet with a rotating base, arranged by size in tiny drawers that were marked, but the dimensions meant nothing to me, so I had to pull each one out to get a look. None of the screws looked like a good match. I chose the best I could find and added a washer and a conical anchor, for which I was charged a quarter. I can't remember the last time an item — much less three items altogether — cost only a quarter. Which was fortunate, as the screw was too small and the conical anchor was too big. The washer worked fine. I managed to find a wood screw in my toolbox and — although it went in a bit slanted — it worked fine, going a little deeper into the hole and so getting into some virgin wood. Far from perfect, but it works. The flap goes up and down with fluid ease, the type of fluidity I associate with fly fishing, the spin of a reel as a threadlike undulation casts out over a stream and a counterfeit fly dimples the surface. Whether a fish bites or not is another story. The flap works. That's what matters.

I forget what's in the paper bag. The one on the edge of the chest of drawers accompanied by a little stuffed Scotsman in a tartan hat who gazes at it wide-eyed with wonder. This has been happening with growing frequency. My memory has been eroding like the cliffs of Normandy, or the little islands disappearing off the coast of Louisiana. I live in mist. My brain is a cloud chamber. There are moments of tremendous clarity regarding the distant past, but whenever I'm preoccupied with something in the present moment — cleaning bathroom tile or writing a haiku — I have a tendency to mislay things, such as racing around frantically looking for my reading glasses only to find them already on my face. I know where everything is in the past. It's the present that feels chaotic and squishy. So what's in the sack? Coppertone, dentifrice, shaving lather, disposable razors, toothpaste, Tylenol and a small plastic travel bottle. Stuff for Kauai. If someone were to tell me that in a few days I'd be entering a machine that will lift me 30,000 feet into the air and carry me to a small island in the Pacific, I'd say they were joking. Or nuts. But that's a tale for the future, which is nothing like the past. The past is a refuge and a burden. The future is garish, like a video game. Until it gets here. Executes a U-turn. And becomes the past.

Remember paper airplanes? Do people still do that? Does that kind of silliness and indolence still exist? Or have the algorithms eaten it? Algorithms don't understand silliness or indolence. They only understand rigorous instructions and data processing. This is not at all like The Beatles. And yet The Beatles keep appearing in my YouTube feed. I am, admittedly, still pretty much hooked on The Beatles. But are the algorithms following me around like big friendly dogs, beagles in love with The Beatles, or are they siloing me further into an echo chamber full of fluffy Peter Max pillows and consumer predictability? Hey algorithms, if you're listening (and of course you're listening) can you begin feeding my indolent gaze with sunset grass and pearls of reason? Can you cure me of logorrhea? Boost my status with ecstatic spider bots and rapid lipstick bees?

Sunak sent to Kyiv to deliver message to Zelenskyy. The Duran. This is at the top of my YouTube feed tonight. Followed by Hound Dog Taylor, Jeremy Spencer, Elmore James and Sophie Hunger. *Le vent nous portera.*

I stare at the computer screen a lot these days. I get floaters in my eyes from the glare. Headaches from all the data. Brain fog from all the propaganda. Must be the season of the witch. Where did I go? It's strange. Sure is strange. You've got to click every link. Listen to inexhaustible podcast jabber. Greece had Socrates. England had Shakespeare. We've got Joe Rogan. It's a weird feeling, this being connected electronically to people. I see very little actual people. And I love conversation. It's almost as hard to find conversation now as it is to find a good movie, or for that matter a theater, or a good restaurant. Hell, a clerk in a music store would be stimulating and fun as a mild psychedelic. It's nice to be in touch with people globally in this faster than lightning medium. The internet can be nice. But it's not Sydney Greenstreet.

We went for a run this afternoon even though it was raining rather heavily. Also, the air quality index on the internet indicated the air was in the moderate, rather than good, range with a score in the 70s. How could this be? It was cold, it was raining, and there were no wildfires. How could the air be bad? Oriana reminded me how stagnant the air had been this last week. Absolutely still. It was weird. Novembers are generally blustery. Winds blast through the region with notable frequency. Not this November. The air was as stagnant as it had been in October, when the summer heat remained, and the sky was tinted with a sulfurous haze. Now, in November, the sky was bluer, but eerily immobile. Today was a shade different. It was too cloudy to see any haze shrouding the city, but the air felt fine. It felt good and smelled good. It had ceased raining and a fine mist tingled on the skin. I was perplexed. The numbers didn't match the actuality. There was a discrepancy between scientific data and sense impressions.

The weather in Kauai today is partly cloudy and 77°. I hope it's that nice when we arrive. And that there will be no delays or cancellations due to snow or fog at Sea-Tac.

This world keeps getting stranger all the time. The era is blunt as a hammer. You either have a lot of money or a lot of debt. No middle-class, no in-between, no buffering milieu of enterprising Rotarians. There are the elites with their billions and the rest of us, with low-paying jobs, shitty benefits, precarious relations, dystopic technology, decaying infrastructure, and chronic anxieties. The barbarity is stark. Homeless encampments outside luxurious compounds. And yet within these harsh parameters there coexist many complexities, intricacies, confusions, and conflicting narratives. No one knows for sure what reality is. Except the truly stupid and arrogant. Yeats got it right: the best lack all conviction, while the worst are full of passionate intensity.

The social fabric has been torn. The monster has risen from his slab of steel and walks awkwardly toward the castle battlements with cruelty in his heart and lightning in his eyes.

It's an odd thing, this mingling of the internal with the external. The objective correlative is a subjective coordinate. Textures, romances, smells. I remember those visits to the lumber yard years ago. The smell of cut wood. The nuclear conundrum of knots. The sawmill in Stendhal.

Vision is the carpenter's balm. Nails are the carpenter's Supreme Court. The juicy iron of the sediment gives his shadow a peach beard. The land begins to cross itself and air out the earth sticks. I think to calculate round by mending a hat. The wind scratches a palm as it approaches the border. The laws here are swooning. Everyone has gone to the moon. What is the mind? Our closet needs commas. I know that because the sauce is sweet tonight. It's high time to invent something for the flaming bohemian in all of us. The restlessness is perfectly normal considering how long it takes for the hour to hatch into daylight. Time is the same everywhere except prison which is a puddle of smashed green water. The fourth dimension is waiting. It's our only hope, a shovel full of almonds in a tincture of lightning. Maybe we can speed it up by tangling away at the chasm. I know a place where the drawers are metal, the offices are whispers and the parabolas rattle with solar winds. The warehouse is to the south. We feel the acute benevolence of angels. I know I'm due to do something, sink into cavernous reflection or go spinning through various careers mixing a savage clarity with the long slow sway of swamp pendulums, which is not going to win me any awards, but it will help with the process of reconciliation, and bring bullets if it fails. Peacocks need plenty of space. I'm getting away if you get interested, and we fly into metallic alloys believing in ourselves even when everyone else has left the room. You be zinc. I'll be brass. And together we'll shine. This could be a song. But it's not. It's a plea for justice. And a field of lavender at the end of a rainbow. The dear coffee of the hardware store will be our fun little elf. They don't call it the nervous system for nothing. It's lonely up here in the percussion section. I have to be able to make thunder when thunder is summoned. And this gives me being. Otherwise I'd be another loop in the woodwinds, an inveterate misdemeanor getting by on regret.

I went to see an audiologist this afternoon. He specialized in tinnitus. Good news for me. I've been plagued with tinnitus for fifty-five years. It started the morning after a catastrophic experience with LSD. It was there when I awoke in a padded room in a hospital in San José, California. It added to the feeling of anxiety and insecurity I was feeling after seeing everything I thought was real dissolve like a cube of sugar in a cup of scalding hot tea.

The audiologist entered the waiting room and invited Oriana and I into his office. He was a large man, chiefly in girth. He reminded me of the comic Louie Anderson who had passed away last January, just a few days before my brother died. He had a genteel, easy-going manner and I felt comfortable around him. He asked a few routine questions concerning my hearing, which Oriana helped corroborate, and the state and history of my tinnitus. After the questions and some further brief discussion he led me down the hall into a small room upholstered with soundproofing foam. The foam was contoured in egg-shaped indentations and bulges and was pleasing to look at. I thought of Proust and his efforts at mitigating the noises of Paris with sound-proofing cork. I told the doctor I'd long dreamed of having such a room.

I was given a set of earphones and the doctor seated himself at a desk in an adjoining room. I could see him through a small glass window. He provided me with a series of sounds, beeps and buzzes and pulses and signals and tones to which I would respond with a "yes" or a "no" or a raise of my hand. One exercise consisted of repeating short sentences as background noises slowly increased. I was worried more about remembering the sentence than hearing the sentence. If I didn't hear the sentence, I didn't have to do anything, but if I heard the sentence I had to repeat it. When we finished, we returned to his office where he showed me a line graph demonstrating that I did, indeed, have significant hearing loss.

The good news was that, yes, a prescription hearing aid would indeed mitigate my tinnitus. He explained how that works: in its attempt to restore the missing input, the auditory neurons in the brain become hyperactive and misfire. This makes the brain become a bit hyperactive. Nerve cells in the dorsal cochlear nucleus go wild with activity. This mayhem of electrical signals may be misinterpreted as a sound, a hiss or whistle or hum. Maybe even music. Since hearing aids restore some of the stimulation that the brain has been missing, they may help reduce the tinnitus. I try to imagine the silence, a silence I've been imagining for fifty-five years, trying to remember what it sounded like, what it felt like. It was the closest I've been to a solution in many ringing jingling hissing humming years. I wanted badly to know what a quiet head would be like before I die. My head will be quiet when I die. But I won't be there to hear it.

I was hoping the doctor might have something on hand to let me see if my tinnitus responded, but he didn't. He went over several of the more helpful products. I was wearing a mask (medical offices still insist on them) so he didn't see the expression of shock on my face when he gave the cost of these items as $5,000 to $7,000. Oriana was similarly stunned. On the way home down dark, depressing Aurora — boarded up motels, used car lots, massage parlors, graffitied walls, sex workers, deserted strip malls — I told Oriana this world isn't for us. It's for the rich.

Hearing aids are gold. More than gold. More like diamond. A modern, RIC BTE (receiver in the canal, behind the ear) hearing aid weighs in at about two grams. It may wholesale for $500 and resale for $2,500. On a per-ounce basis, that's a staggering $7,200 at wholesale and $36,000 at resale. For comparison, gold is currently trading around $1,600 an ounce. In other words, hearing aids cost over twenty times their weight in gold.

They say silence is gold. I'd say it's worth more than that. It's hard to find silence in this world. When silence is denied due to a ringing in the head you have to look for it elsewhere. In the nails of an old mailbox. In the tread of a tractor that passed by yesterday. In a poem. In the chill air under a dock. Silence becomes something imagined. Behind the ringing there's a silence. If you could hear it, it wouldn't be silence. It would be ringing. Ringing isn't silence. Ringing is what makes silence silent. Ringing is the sound of silence. It isn't silence. It's the shadow of silence.

What would I do if I had a moment of silence? I would do what I always do. I would visit the tamarind cat planetarium. I'd wear an archaic bandage of real character. I'd whistle tunes to my shirt. I'd tangle up an area in female percussion. Because I'm on the verge. I'm on the verge of something. Rubbing arms with the old wheel of smell in the stars. It could use some soap.

I'm going to hone a catastrophe. I need to get my brain working. My hummingbird gallantry and its exquisite savagery requires the jelly of metaphor. Cardboard worms. Mycelium and silt. Buffalo Bill and his Wild West Show. All the hornets in my knee attack the dogmatism of wax. My neurons are lost in a song. Think of this as a book written with a purposeful purposelessness. A dreamy abstraction bending your head.

I employ a special light for my experiments. The lab gets so dark at times. The darkness has a voice. I made another one out of crumpled beer cans and paddled it with a shoulder blade.

I stay away from challenges. I simply don't like them. I prefer walking down country roads smelling the rain just before it begins falling. The heart of the heartwood is in the knot of its comedy.

Not everything is about turtlenecks. Or Tin Pan Alley. Some things require a little balance, a little consciousness. It's all about ski lifts and gnostic dwarfs in the forests of Norway. I don't know why else anyone would bother to remove their ambivalence. Everything else is boring as fuck. I like putting words together so that they create the skill of failure. It's the most important skill I have. I can't take a brain apart and improve its functioning. But I can stuff it with words. And the more words there are circulating in the brain, the more ways there are to alter reality.

These are the words I meant to put here. They're stepping into the void. They could be anywhere. Or maybe they didn't go anywhere at all. They're right here. These are the words. The very words by which I meant to say something. Which otherwise had been a place to go. And now they're here. Ebony and agate. The splendor of obsidian eyes. I will say nothing that will implicate me in your private life. I've never been there. I hear it's beautiful. Perhaps you could send me a post card. Who are you, by the way?

The blind see clearer because they're blind, ironizes Denis Diderot. And in walks Bob Dylan with a Stratocaster. He can see where he's going because this is Nashville, and it's dark. I'm telling you there's a strong wind coming so you'd better keep a bookmark handy. Aquariums are fun but London real estate can make me crave fireballs of semantic instability. Why is water so infrared at the top of your spine? Beware of the enema within. Here's what I love about the English language: endoplasmic reticulum, participles, idioms, and cream puffs. Try it somewhere warm. We will be words together chained to a cross on a Broadway stage. This is how thinking begins. There's nothing concrete to grab hold of, and the hamster wheel goes all night.

You can smell it: Keith Richards walking the streets of Mandeville late at night. Above and below have no meaning in space. And this is true of anything. Sometimes an electron can literally be nowhere. And nowhere is fine. It's where crickets create adjectives. I hear a roar in the sky. And then I hear rain. All the mannequins are dead. Naked and dead. Because no one has bothered to clothe them. I forget what it was I came here to say. Don't let future employers see this. Life is so quiet without people. There's consciousness in everything. One must act to give oneself existence. Like those toads in the road. It's easy to create a new reality. All you need is a little clay, some salsa, a bright and wonderful day in Memphis, and the keys to the hardware store.

We live in a serious world. Sooner or later, the implications begin talking.

This is Danny Kirwan wandering the streets of London in 1995.

This is Geoffrey Chaucer wandering the streets of London in 1387.

This is Crazy Horse wading the Yellowstone in 1864.

This is a drop of trust wide-eyed with excitement.

This is the crash required to achieve a certain rapport with distance. These are levers to pull while speaking of coffee. This the art of washing a tamarind. This is the expandability of a book inspired by wind.

Farts. If you want to think of it that way. Me, I'd go with a different sentiment, something complicated like a machine. But where is the consciousness of a machine? Is it in the machine? Is it a sense? Is it a submarine sending signals under the waters of Greenland? Let's call it a day and go home. Which is a stone's throw from the universe on the other side of your eyes.

Fun facts about eyes: the human eye can differentiate approximately ten million colors, is made up of over two million working parts, and is the fastest muscle in the body. Hence the phrase: in the blink of an eye. If you're reading this, I'm guessing you're using a pair of eyes. Your own, I hope. I've tried seeing things through the eyes of other people and it just makes me want to go hide under the bed. Or sit in darkness.

The retina is pivotal. The retina changes light into electrical impulses which are then sent through the optic nerve to the brain and turned into the images that we see.

The mist of nails is mixed with phosphor. But this is not the heading I want to demonstrate. What I intended was struggle. An exhausted swimmer walking toward a tug. Is the tug adrift? This depends on one's position regarding stencils. Is life a tour, or more like the canals of Venice? If we're going to consider alternatives, there's always a commotion. Always a conflict. People will argue about anything. And now that we're on the eighty-yard line with no time out, I can see the end zone and hear the crowd cry out. We're in the realm of the punt. The ignition of my morality depends on the ballast of my sneakers. I love to play salt. Buttermilk is a loopy substance. And thereby hangs a wheel. It's time for my daily spin.

Oriana and I return from a run around the top of Queen Anne. Lots of hungry crows out today. We brought four bags of peanuts. Toss a peanut to one crow and in half a second twelve to thirteen more appear. I stop to look at a sign laminated and stapled to a telephone pole. It says:

HELLO FRIEND. I'm a night blooming jasmine. Thank you for enjoying my flowers for over twenty years. I hope you're not dead. Death was never my intent. I was aiming for fragrance combined with goose bumps, the kind you get at night, when the first drag queen appears on the stage. Dolly Parton. Patsy Cline. Queen Elizabeth. It's another cathedral hive Monday. I'm sinking into music. The world pendulum is seeking an orchard in which to swing. We looked everywhere for it all the clubs on Beale Street and even the bakery over on Mount Moriah Road. Why do pilots travel in knots? Come on baby rock with me. You know I feel good. When the spirit hits me I shake all over. Like Jerry Lee Lewis in an echo chamber. Like a reel of film in the wrong projector. Like a reel of film in the right projector. Who's to blame if I can't feel a thing? Who's to blame if I feel everything? The knot is a unit of speed that ties directly into the global latitude and longitude coordinate system and is therefore easier to navigate with. I'm a knot not done until I'm undone. Said the guzzle to the thunder claw. The polar shovel is full of apricots. It's a Limestone All Things Music Pancake Tuesday. It takes more than a little aggression to translate the world as a heavily foliated evergreen shrub. It takes a sky of poplar canaries and a high fun road of emboldened jeep bandits. A flirtation with Navajo. And a deep long gulp of Papiamentu.

Papiamentu is a Portuguese-based creole language. It tastes like metamorphosis on the end of a stick. A chrysalis breaking open and a butterfly emerging in a dance of aerial silk. In other words, strawberry kiwi banana with a hint of milk.

Not to mention Pessoa. What's he up to today? Disquiet. Yes. There's that.

I'm feeling dizzy. I'm trying to catch up with the life I felt behind when I went to Kauai for five days. Five days is all takes to lose track of things. I'm back on the treadmill of indecision. Should I get hearing aids? They're astronomically expensive. And not covered by my healthcare plan. If I get a hearing aids, will I need a smartphone? I dread smartphones. I see what they do to people. That's an issue to pursue when I have time to elaborate my arguments. All of them impotent. Right now I'm just dizzy. That life I've been leading took me right to the precipice. The view is fantastic. But it's a long way down. And the rocks are basaltic and black. And eternity rides the horizon, silent and blue and endless and cruel. And is making me dizzy.

A lot of this has to do with first being relieved of one's respon-sibilities, the decisions that have to be made, burdens assumed, frustrations chafed, queries answered, nagging household repairs accomplished, appointments scheduled, hassles upon hassles upon hassles, all that separated from you for a few days, maybe months, and then you're back, unpacking a suitcase, or putting it off till tomorrow, or petting a puzzled cat. I don't have a smart-phone, so once I'm disconnected, I'm truly disconnected. That might not be an option for a lot of people now. No wonder they're so grouchy materialistic and superficial. Their brains have been eaten by a monster called AI.

When you get home, all of it comes tumbling down like shoe-boxes and photo albums in overstuffed closets. When the astro-nauts return to Earth they always look so funny, so flaccid and rubbery they can't walk. They've been floating in weightlessness for six months or more. That's how it feels. You're no longer weightless. You're getting pressed down by this thing called grav-ity. Called existence. Called survival. Called angst. Called pour me a glass of wine.

Also, the bill. Expenses incurred during a trip are all added up and wrapped in the cold uncaring language of mathematics and all those sweet lobby smiles are given a monetary value.

How much does paradise cost? $1,100 per day. And it broke my camera.

The last picture I took was a monkey pod tree in Moir Gardens, Kauai. Long Brobdingnagian limbs ramifying into a universe of its own making. Too much, apparently, for a small digital appa-ratus collecting photons with Grundy sensors.

A month or so ago I was trying to find a carrying case and strap for my Bose earphones. Earphones are crucial. I need music. I need protection against crying babies and loud voices. I enjoy disappearing into a world of dramas and funny cat videos and Jimmy Dore on YouTube. Brick and mortar stores have all but gone extinct so I have to order everything on Amazon. Then wait and hope it shows up before we leave. Music is my heroin. My balm. My uplift in life.

I've listened to so many songs now on YouTube, songs I still love, but do get a little tired of hearing if I listen to them too much and too repeatedly, that the old music of the Renaissance and Baroque begin to sound fresher than the music of the 1960s and 1970s, which was my era. And not so new, it's true. It's been fifty years at least. Amazes me it still gets played a lot. Grocery stores, restaurants, bars. The music faded as it was eaten by the music business. The gluttony of profit. A lot of the good stuff, new or old, blends together well. Segues from the Bohemian-Austrian composer Heinrich Ignaz Franz Biber to the Beach Boys or Beatles or Etta James sounds completely natural. Procul Harem's "Whiter Shade of Pale" was based on Bach's "Air on a G String." Beck's "Bolero" was inspired by Ravel's "Bolero." Can's "Soul Desert" is ancient incantation.

I also bought a T-shirt at Pike Place Market. It's hot in Kauai. I can't walk around in a ratty white T-shirt. I bought a black T-shirt with a picture in white of an octopus wrapping its tentacles around the helmet of a deep-sea diver whose caption read "There's a Monster Down There," and a small notebook with a pattern of crows on a cream background that fits in my breast pocket.

Six days ago, on a cold November morning, Oriana performed her magic on her smartphone and contacted an Uber driver to pick us up and drive us to Sea-Tac.

The driver got to our driveway so fast it seemed preternatural. We put our roller suitcase into the trunk and off we went. The driver's name was Odhiambo and he was from Nairobi, Kenya. We had a good conversation on the way to the airport. We talked about how long each of us had lived in Seattle, rampant inflation, floods and draughts and tornados, contrasts in weather, and Léopold Sédar Senghor, poet and first president of the Republic of Senegal.

As soon as we entered the airport I felt overwhelmed, disoriented and discombobulated by the crowds, the gates, the cordoned off areas, the signs and numbers, the grim security guards. We did some walking — walking — and more walking, until we found the proper line to stand in, which was ginormous. I'd never seen a line that long. It had to have been over a half mile, at least. It wound round and round a series of divider ropes. Everyone looked bored and weary.

We made it through security, all the hoops they use to confuse and humiliate you. I find myself to stymied by the stupidity of it all I go numb inside. I had to fill three trays rapidly with clothes, satchel, tablet, keys and wallet, shoes and glasses and pen and notebook. The little spiral on the notebook alone might trigger an alarm and I'd be surrounded by an armed SWAT team.

I got frisked, rubbed down by a total stranger, a big guy with red hair who looked me over like a cockroach. He was probably just sick of rubbing people hour after hour. It's a moronic ritual. I keep my jokes about it to myself. You either comply, or you don't get on the plane. No wonder fights break out on planes. Everyone has been rendered so impotent and foolish. It was like being in prison, at the mercy of the guards. And this is supposed to make you feel secure?

As soon as we made it to our gate and got settled, Oriana went off for some coffee and breakfast. I stayed behind to watch our luggage. She returned with a concoction of yogurt and fruit and two maple bars for me. I love patisserie. But I felt I needed something with actual nutrition. I asked where Oriana got the fruit and yogurt and she pointed in the direction of the little open food mart we'd passed on the way to the gate. I went in search of a fruit cup. Couldn't find it. I went to the cash register where two East African woman worked as cashiers dressed in black abaya. I told them I was looking for a fruit cup. They had no idea what I was talking about. Nor did they seem over-concerned. I returned to our seat. Oriana told me I went to the wrong food mart. She pointed to the right one, closer by, where some loud thumpity-thump dance music was providing some accompaniment to my headache. I couldn't find it there either. I wasn't looking for the right thing. Oriana was eating a concoction of yogurt, granola, and fruit that came as a single kit. I hadn't been paying attention when she assembled it. I went back and got one. I didn't care for it much (I hate granola) but it served to insure a healthier fuel for a seventy-five-year-old body running on antidepressants, antacid tablets and bile.

We got an announcement that a mechanic had discovered a hydraulic leak on our plane. They would have to replace the plane. This would take about two hours. I got my tablet out and hooked up to the airport wi-fi and listened to a talk on France Culture Radio titled *"Le Loup: Un Ami Devenu Ennemi"* ("The Wolf: A Friend Become an Enemy"). I learned that 46,000 years ago, approximately, wolves followed Cro Magnon groups around to eat the scraps of fallen prey, mastodons, cave bears, horses and reindeer. The dynamic was mutually beneficial, as the wolves, with keener powers of smell and hearing were able to warn *Homo*

: 133 :

sapiens when danger was near, and fought off predators such as lions and leopards. Eventually, the wolves — chiefly injured and older wolves too old to hunt — approached the humans and became domesticated into dogs, chihuahuas to rottweilers to border collies. Wolf-dogs could track and harass elk and bison until the prey weakened from fatigue. Then the Homo sapiens could kill the prey more easily with spears or bows and arrows. Wolves benefited from this as well, as the humans shared the meat with them. wolf-dogs would have tracked and harassed animals like elk and bison and would have hounded them until they tired. Then humans would have finished them off with spears or bows and arrows. It was a win-win situation.

Each time a door opened to a passenger boarding bridge we felt a blast of cold air. We looked for a place to move to, but it was too crowded; all the seats had been taken. It was a huge relief when the time to board our plane arrived. This is a fun part, entering a plane and maneuvering down a narrow aisle (much narrower than in the past) and heaving our suitcase into the overhead compartment and squeezing past our seatmate on the aisle and sitting down. The space was much more cramped than in the past. Clearly, amenities have diminished over the years.

Our seatmate was a man in his forties wearing little else than a T-shirt and short pants. He had large hairy legs and bushy brown hair. He seemed friendly, but as our flight got underway he immersed himself in his smartphone and laptop and he made it all too apparent he wasn't up for any conversation, not even a little introductory banter. It was remarkable. I'd never experienced behavior like this before. I wasn't sure what to make of it.

The roar of the engines and ascension into the sky is always a thrill. I love this part of flight.

I successfully linked to the airplane's wi-fi, but couldn't get any internet service. I tried repeatedly. It just wasn't going to happen. This is a huge disappointment. I was a bilious misanthrope with a bad case of hyperacusis vulnerable to the loud cries of multiple babies and overexcited and disgruntled children. The earphones I'd gone to all the trouble of bringing to protect against this scenario were useless. Nor did the plane offer any movies; I pulled the tray down expecting to see a movie screen, but there was nothing. I spent the flight cramped, miserable, headachy, stealing occasional glances at my seatmate's laptop. One of the more intriguing shows was called (as I found out later) *The Peripheral*, a sci-fi streaming television series available on Amazon Prime in which a VR gamer is "delivered a connection to an alternate reality, as well as a dark future of her own." I watched as a handsome, bearded man cut meat in a chi-chi kitchen as another tough-looking old guy snuck up from behind with a knife. A young woman zaps the would-be assassin with a taser-like device and the assassin fell to the floor in a convulsive seizure.

I turned the other way and glanced out the window. I saw some of the strangest cloud formations I'd ever seen, clouds in columns, like monoliths of turquoise mist. The toddler in the seat behind me continued kicking my seat. His parents looked vacant and faraway. *Non compos mentis*. Complaining to them would not lead to happy results.

I'd brought three books with me, *L'amour fou* by André Breton and *Mad Love*, an English translation by Mary Ann Caws in case I got stumped on a sentence or phrase (my French dictionary was too large to fit in my valise, which also carried a small digital camera), and *A Draft of XXX Cantos* by Ezra Pound. Pound was there to keep my mind alert and active. Breton was there to take me elsewhere. They were good choices.

I'd also brought the October, 2022 issue *Philosophie* magazine to which Oriana subscribed as a Christmas present every year. Each issue was devoted to a particular theme. This one was *La sobriété: pourquoi est-il si difficile de se modérer?* (Sobriety: Why Is It So Difficult to Moderate Oneself). There was a feature on the Ethics of Baruch Spinoza which included a thin booklet stapled into the magazine. I packed the magazine in the suitcase where I couldn't reach it. No matter. Breton's *L'amour fou* helped transport me from a passenger jet to a haven of reverie.

Breton is all about *dépaysement*, exploring foreign lands, not literal lands but imaginative domains, continents of altered perception, the sameness of things ripped into semantic confusion, places where the mind can open itself to stunning accidents drunk on chance, on spontaneity, on amber candor, on ambiguity, the hint of blue light in a cave of crystal and unusual silicates of fumarolic sublimates. Depictions on the walls of the world above: elk, bear, bison, wolf. Fish in meandering transparencies of dream, as if dream were the dilation of a membrane, a wormhole undulating like a moon jellyfish. Breton's sentences are both fluid and evocative. For a time, he proofread for Proust and that wonderful Proustian music is there too, rippling along in sweet reveries. Words are sperm in ovarian aquariums. The syntax wiggles, trembles because it's a living chain of alluring twists and fugitive thoughts. It was the perfect thing to read while feeling cramped in a jet airliner passenger seat, the back of which was getting kicked by a two-year-old.

Oriana read Melville's *Omoo: A Narrative of Adventures in the South Seas* on her tablet. She loved his writing. It was so lushly detailed, a wealth of expression surging in vivid, sensory vitality from the beauty of its words.

I'd never been so eager to spot land. This was a new experience. I mistook cloud formations for land so often that when land did finally appear, I wasn't entirely sure it was land until the pilot made a formal announcement that we were approaching our destination. There would soon be an end to my torture.

At 7:30 P.M. (Seattle time) we slid down through the humid tropical mist — already tinged and opalescent with moonlight — and hit the tarmac hard. I wondered how the ninety-three-year-old woman a few seats up responded to that. She required help disembarking. Kauai was on her bucket list. This was a place she felt the need to visit one last time before leaving her wrecked and decrepit body. I could understand this completely. There was something heroic about it.

Once we got in the airport Oriana lost no time contacting a Lyft driver. We raced to an assigned area for ride service vehicles, essentially three or four slots in a parking lot with a roundabout occupied by a large monkey pod tree. Our driver was a large man, I'm guessing in his fifties, who'd been a weather reporter on Hawaiian TV and was now teaching eighth grade science in a local junior high. He had a beautiful voice, deep and mellow. He described all the things we'd be seeing if it had been day-light (the density of shadowy trees strongly intimated a very lush forest) and the difficulties of educating children. Reading skills had radically declined. This never fails to demoralize me and increase my anxiety. The lack of literacy assumes visible and troubling form. There was a thump. This had been a frog. I could tell our driver felt bad. But what can you do? I would soon discover the corpses of frogs smashed into the pavement nearly everywhere. It had been years since I'd seen a frog. I wasn't even sure they still existed.

We arrived at our hotel and the driver helped retrieve our suit-case from the back. We bid goodnight and he drove off into the warm sultry night. And here we were. Lush warm air caressing our tired bodies and the sound of the Pacific pounding beaches of brown sugar sand.

We entered the lobby and — apart from the confusion of see-ing a Christmas tree and Christmas decorations on what I'd already assumed was summer — I was puzzled as to whether I was standing inside or outside. I was outside. There was a large open space where I could see a few stars.

The clerk at the desk was a pleasant thirty-something Hawai-ian woman in a dress peppered (or would it be peopled) with orchids. She checked us in and handed us a map of the complex to help find our room, and a box of complementary macadamia nut chocolates. There didn't appear to be any bellhops around. It took us less than five minutes to get utterly lost, and another ten minutes to find our room. We were both extremely tired and disoriented. Seasons were turned upside down and somewhere between the continental United States and this tiny island I'd lost my sense of direction.

After we found our room — a very pleasant and large room with a balcony overlooking the Pacific — and deposited our belongings on several chairs we went out to get dinner at the hotel restaurant, Lava's on Poipu Beach. The airline had only served — in two intervals — a tiny bag of pretzels and several hours later a package of two small graham crackers. A cheerful waitress appeared and led us to a table outside. We gazed at the menu some time and the waitress returned. I ordered a Tog-arashi Meatloaf, two "4 oz beef meatloaf slices rubbed with togarashi spice, served with fried Brussels sprouts, mushroom gravy, and mashed potatoes." Oriana ordered a Chilled Ahi Soba Noodle Salad, "seared rare ahi rubbed with togarashi sliced thin and served on a soba noodle salad with carrot, red pepper, red onions, and sesame." Both dinners were fantastic. Absolutely delicious. Lava's on Poipu Beach turned out to be a gem.

On our walk back to our room, we realized, for the first time, the immensity of ocean that minute by minute tumbled onto spits and jetties of black basaltic rock, thick white undulating turbulences of foam appearing almost phosphorescent under a night sky in which a full moon glowed in a halo of noctilucent clouds. It was breathtaking.

Oriana went looking for the box of macadamia nut chocolates. It was missing. She was certain she'd put it on the bureau under the big-screen TV. I couldn't remember seeing her doing it, I'd been so distracted by the amenities of the room, the moonlit Pacific, and sheer fatigue from all the stress of TSA agents and crying babies and monotony of clouds and the unfolding of a refractory and incomprehensible distance.

We got up early in the morning and went for a run down Hoonani Road and back. It was a shorter run than I'd planned on doing but without a map it was hard to figure out a route in which we wouldn't get lost. I left my compass back in my valise.

We heard roosters crowing. This is a curious feature of the island. Hundreds of wild chickens run wild as though there'd never existed anything like a coop or a farm or bipedal simi-ans driving two-ton cars. The roosters were gorgeous: a palette of fiery discordances, iridescent red, persimmon, neon yellow, a bit of blue, jet-black tail feathers arcing in uncompromising verve. It was a novelty to hear them all crowing every morning (it reminded me of my grandparent's farm in North Dakota) but four days later I wanted to strangle each and every one of them.

We showered and got dressed and went for some breakfast at Lava's. It was crowded. Lots of families with kids. This puzzled me. Why weren't the kids in school? I'm a bit like W. C. Fields around kids. "Anybody who hates children and dogs can't be all bad." I do love dogs. It's their owners that give me pause. We were seated and offered coffee and orange juice. I love orange juice. It's like sunlight in the mouth. It never fails to perk me up. And it's great with coffee. The waiter returned and took our orders. Oriana ordered the Loco Moco (4 oz wagyu beef patty, over-easy egg, sticky rice, hamakua mushrooms, scallions, pickled red onions, red wine beef gravy, sriracha aioli) and I ordered the Red Velvet French Toast (with a vanilla cheesecake filling and banana maple syrup) but they were out of toast, so I got the Rise and Grindz (pan fried soy-ginger Spam, sunny-side up egg, furikake sticky rice). Both were knockouts. Tasty postulates of hyperbolic food. I was feeling quantum. Anomalous and frequent. Good food does this to me.

It feels good to be anomalous. Anonymously anomalous. It's best to be anomalous when you're not drawing attention to yourself. Anonymity is a luxury. Like being a chameleon. Deviation makes people nervous. They don't know what to expect. It puts them on their guard. The current zeitgeist is especially nervous about anomalies. Different perceptions lead to different narratives, a healthy skepticism toward the dominant narratives of one's time. This can be exhausting. It can make one world-weary, and lonely. An anomalous disposition is invigorating so long as it is disguised by a pleasant smile and a casual demeanor. Food is comforting. It allows one's anomalies to bloom in blithe anonymity, the way of all exotic plants and flowers.

We watched the sparrows fly into the restaurant — which was entirely open to the world, the Pacific and its eternal churn — and peck at remnants of food, bread crumbs and rice. The waiters bussed the tables so the food would remain fair game for a few minutes before it was cleared away. We love birds, we feed crows at home, so this was some pleasant amusement while we waited for the check. That, and watching the surfers. There was also a swimmer, a guy in a wet suit, who swam back and forth the entire time we ate breakfast. His stamina was amazing. I'm guessing the wet suit was for protection against the jellyfish. The water was quite warm.

We decided to hike to Makauwahi Cave. Makauwahi Cave is Kauai's largest limestone cave and is an archeological treasure. It's chock-a-block with fossils: forty to fifty types of birds, including the nocturnal and endangered Laysan duck, the turtle-jawed and flightless moa-nalo goose, an extinct nearly blind mole duck (*Talpanas lippa*) with a flat skull and tiny wings that probably fed on forest insects, artifacts of bone and coral, iron nails and goat teeth, a long-legged owl, a new species of bat, blind wolf spiders (still residing within the cave) seed pods and pollen from the kanaloa shrub, whose two known surviving members cling to Kaho'olawe cliffs, fragments of Polynesian pottery, fishing hooks and braided fishing line, canoe fragments and pipipi picks. The pipipi snail's shell makes a good ukulele pick. It was also used for bracelets and necklaces.

Makauwahi means — roughly — "smoke hole." This may have been in reference to shamanic practices of a kahuna — a Hawaiian priest, sorcerer, magician, wizard or enlightened savant — such as reading omens and prophecies in the smoke spiraling up from a fire, or spodomancy, divination by examining ashes.

We went in search of the two-mile coastal trail from Shipwrecks beach. We could find no trace of it. Somehow, we'd managed to find ourselves at the intersection of Hoowili Road and Poipu Road. An older man on a mountain bike rode toward us when I waved, hoping he might know the name of the street where we were standing. Road signs seem to be something of a rarity on the island. He didn't. The hotel chains here were new. I don't know whether it's a matter of body language or appearance or vibes but eccentrics and misfits always manage to spot a fellow maverick. I could tell by his seasoned and craggy face he had been living on the island for some time. We told him how lucky he must be to live in such a place. He said it was the first few years but after a while it's just another place. Like they say in AA, wherever you go there you are. He did seem a little morose and disenchanted. Maybe it was all the development. Or the general mayhem and lunacy of the current moment. On that note we bid adieu and he went on his way.

It was extremely hot and I was already dying of thirst. There was a market down the road where I could get some bottled water and maybe a map. Oriana surrendered to the exigency of the moment and contacted a Lyft driver, a man in his fifties who reminded me a little of *Jurassic Park* actor Sam Neil. I hoped there would be a place where I could get some water near the cave, a water fountain or a little grocery store. Life is an ongoing study in contrasts. Outside was paradise, swaying palms and exotic birds, but it was all scorpions and cacti and Death Valley in my mouth. The driver said there was a horse ranch near the cave. I wasn't sure what that indicated as far as getting a drink of water, but it put the possibility of water on the table.

The driver took us up a long dirt road whose dust and clay were a solid russet. There were a lot of potholes and craters. Oriana apologized and — when we went as far as we could — gave him an extra twenty dollars to wash his car.

There was no water available, only a puddle of very maroon water. We continued on our way. Maybe there'd be water of some sort at the cave.

We followed the trail to a small hole leading into a rock. It seemed a bit dubious, but we got down on our knees and crawled through. Some cardboard had been placed on the ground, but I managed to get an adhesive claylike russet on the knees of my pants. We exited into a large amphitheater of limestone and palm trees. I looked up at the rim where Johnny Depp had taken a leap in *Pirates of the Caribbean.*

The mouth of the cave was enormous. I looked into its darkness expecting to see a kahuna emerge waving a palm frond on the back of a giant tortoise. Or a dinosaur sleeping, curled up in a corner, the membranous flutter of a rhythmic snore. I entered and the air cooled immediately. There was a park guide nearby — a gracious young woman named Layla (I'm guessing her parents were Eric Clapton fans) who discussed some of the critical issues pertaining to the preservation of the cave and the surrounding ecology, much of which had already been seriously damaged, such as a nearby creek which was polluted after a resident tried diverting the stream away from his property. Developers pretty much dominated everything and corruption infiltrated all the strata of local governing bodies. She also recommended a book about the cave and its fossils called *Back to the Future in the Caves of Kauai* by David A. Burney.

I asked if there were any water available. Just what she had in the water pitcher she'd brought for herself, but she kindly offered to pour some in the plastic lid, along with a couple of ice cubes. The water was cold and refreshing. There's a special relief that comes with a drink of water when you're seriously dehydrated, a sportive euphoria. I thanked her and put a twenty dollar bill into a glass donation jar.

We began our walk back to Poipu Road. The dirt road and horse ranch reminded me North Dakota. It was an odd pairing of two vastly different climates and geographies. Most of life is like that. Moral codes and sanctuaries cross-eyed as a lynx in a cubbyhole. If it doesn't make sense, give it a kiss and let it go. And if it does make sense, more power to you. A shaggy old man in a pickup roared by and stopped and asked it we wanted to hop on the tailgate for a ride. I said sure and off we went. It was bumpy but welcome. I was tired, discombobulated and thirsty. As we approached what appeared to be a luxury hotel Oriana banged on the bed of the truck with her hand the man came to a stop. We hopped off and I thanked him and off he went in a cloud of russet dust.

Oriana suggested we look for some water in the luxury hotel, but I said it was futile. These places don't have water fountains anymore. I don't think you're going to find anything in there except suspicious looks and goddesses in sunglasses. But off she went, determined as Roald Amundsen. Several minutes went by. I went to look for her. I entered a cavernous lobby and looked down two halls, one going north the other going south. No sign of Oriana. I looked outside. She wasn't there either. Then I spotted her, walking down a hall at a fast pace. I shouted and got her attention. Just as I thought, there wasn't any water here. But there was outside. There was a small table with a big pitcher of water on it and paper cups. This was for the valets. We went over and helped ourselves to a drink. I was wrong. The place did have some water.

We walked back down to Poipu Road. We could hear the screech of a scaly breasted munia coming from the partially wooded golf course across the road while Oriana requested a Lyft driver on her smartphone. The effect of that last drink didn't last long. I still craved water.

While we waited, Oriana checked our email on her smartphone. The catsitter, an amiable soul with a great sense of humor and a good listener — a longtime friend we met some years ago when we were looking for a catsitter for our other beloved cat Octave who had passed away some years ago — kindly sent pictures of our cat Molly twice a day. We worried horribly about Molly. This was the first time we had left her alone. We were extremely attached, and an acute current of separation anxiety tinged even the most paradisiacal moments. It was especially calming to hear she was eating and letting our catsitter stroke her under her chin, distressing when the only picture she could get was that of Molly hiding under the bed, her two green eyes aglow in the dark. Why is she hiding under dark, I asked. Do you think it's the guy upstairs making a lot of noise? Cats do that when they're stressed, Oriana answered. They find a hideaway.

We had a casual dinner at a popular diner called Bubba's. Afterward, we stopped in at Long's Drugstore and bought four big bottles of water. When we returned to our hotel, in between reading books and checking email, I drank water. In gulps. In slurpy sips. In swigs and swills. In abandon and immoderation. Hours later things shifted in my body and three days of constipation reversed itself and became as fatiguing in endless visits to the can as a colonoscopy prep.

If you're sitting on a toilet, you're not in paradise. There are no toilets in paradise. And if the receptionist is a young woman in a Hawaiian dress peppered with orchids, this may also be a sign you're not in paradise. You may be in a tropical island hotel lobby with Christmas decorations and warm soothing air and not know the distinction between inside and outside. You're close to paradise. But the entry remains elusive. And is contingent. On what, nobody knows. Except a few prophets, healers and shamans. And the line at the ocean's horizon which reveals a slight curve. Meaning you're on a planet. It's not paradise. But it could be. Minus hotels and tourists. And a gazillion chickens. Who appear as confused as you are.

Next morning, after completing a short run, I went down to the ocean feeling the cool brown sugar sand on my feet and waded into the ocean and floated there a minute or two. The water was warm. I could've floated there all day. I was even beginning to wonder if we'd have time for some surfing lessons, something I hadn't done since Santa Cruz in the summer of 1966. It was early morning November 30th.

We went for breakfast at Lava's, and once again the food was terrific. We watched a man out on the waves press up and down on a surfboard, which caused it to go faster, and provided more liberty to go where he wanted. It had a shaft underneath with wings at its base which boosted the hydrodynamic qualities of the surfboard. As the board moves forward, the wings lift it out of the water. Gliding above the surface allows for tighter turns due to the smaller surface area in contact with the water. But I remain puzzled as to how all that pumping made it go faster.

We decided to take a walk out to Spouting Horn Park. Spouting Horn is a blowhole in a mass of lava rock on the coastline. Erosion has formed tunnels within the rock and when a big wave comes smashing into it the water it's forced through the tunnel and out through the blowhole in a column of mist. The sound this makes is a bit eerie. It sounds like the bellowing and hissing of a huge monster whose giant lungs routinely expel rage and frustration into the sweet Pacific air. According to legend, the coastline was once guarded by a giant lizard named Kaikapu who would eat anyone who tried to fish or swim in the area. A boy named Liko dove under the ocean to outwit Kaikapu but the monster was quick-witted and attacked the boy, who threw a sharp stick into Kaikapu's mouth and swam under the lava shelf. From there, he escaped through a small hole to the surface. Kaikapu tried to follow but got stuck. To this day, you can hear the monster's roar and breath spraying from the blowhole in high columns of ocean mist. I was a little underwhelmed by it, but found a vacant picnic table to sit down and enjoy the breezes cooling my skin and lulling a weary world into swaying palms and quiescent assent. War was unthinkable in a setting such as this. What this place articulated so well was a swirl of pleasing sensations, the comforting murmur of waves crashing, pounding refractory rock, the infinite space at the horizon line, the shimmer of palm fronds, the lush foliage of the mountains and hills, the feeling of cosmic benevolence that imbued the humid air and opened one's pores and spirit. Oriana busied herself taking pictures of the blowhole spray. She got some really good ones.

I've never been much suited for photography. I'm more of a dreamer. Dials and aperture settings confuse me. My digital camera was pretty easy to use, it made all the adjustments automatically, but it still required some skill and attention, which is a slightly different mindset than vacancy. I'm hooked on that feeling of diffusion that comes over you in those rare moments when you can let everything go and empty yourself into the void. It's a luxury. A self-induced heroin of the soul.

We've all got a talent for something. Mine has always been day-dreaming. Woolgathering. Tripping. Going in and out of fugue states. I was never meant for third base. My favorite position in Little League was left field. They put me in left field for good reason, and I've been there ever since.

I'm the Errol Flynn of reverie. My favorite activity is inactivity. I love the action of inaction. The inclination to recline in a wine of idleness. The beatitude of latitude in a desuetude of lassitude.

The one big exception to this is running. I love to run. The really great discovery that day was finding a good trail to run on: Hoonani Road to Lawai Road to the Spouting Horn Blowhole and back.

We walked back to our hotel with a brief stop at Long's Drugstore. I was too hot and wet to go inside so I waited outside in the shade of the awning. I watched as a large woman who must've been in her late eighties or early nineties hobbled by with the assistance of an aide. She wore a big loose dress with a floral print. Her legs were splotched and bloated and scaly and yet she'd gone to the trouble of painting her toenails dark red.

I noticed a lot of elderly people — permanent residents I'm guessing — whose skin had been ravaged by the sun. The equatorial sun is intense, high in ultraviolet rays which have less distance to travel through the atmosphere. I saw women in stylish beach clothes who looked like mummies. Healthy, though; a lot of them were riding bikes.

We passed two memorials on our walk, signs under which a mound of gifts and flowers had been strewn, one for a young, extremely popular woman in her thirties who drowned while performing her vocation as an underwater photographer, and another at a more distant location along Lawai Road, a woman in her fifties, also beloved, who'd been murdered. No one was sure what had happened. He body had been discovered in a state of considerable decomposition. The woman was characterized as fun-loving and friendly, though had, it had been noted somewhat vaguely, some conflicts with people. I found these intriguing. The enchantment of this island, although manifestly benign, hadn't completely cured the human animal of its propensity to violence.

Some of the finest moments of this trip were spent on the balcony of our hotel. It was still and quiet and I could sit and read and occasionally take a look through the binoculars at a party on the stern of a catamaran or a lone surfer way out on the water waiting for a wave. The horizon was a continual fascination. So empty of anything except its own illusory line, it subtly revealed the curvature of the planet and the monotonous shimmer of eternity between two shades of blue.

I began writing haiku. I hadn't written haiku in years. Here's a few I call Poipu Haiku:

> it's absorbing how
> the sequential grace of each wave
> leaves the moon behind

> grains of sand
> caught in the grooves of the sliding door
> in archipelagos

black swan
in the pond by the hotel ringed
by a frenzy of goldfish

the furious paddling
to surf the moment a wave
lifts into chaos

binoculars
on open horizon, I see
blue glitter forever

impromptu
memorial for a woman
murdered in paradise

what is "the"
doing in a roar, does the ocean's voice
need such framing?

Spinoza's Ethics
interrupted by a woman
clacking her sandals

I continued to fuss with my tablet to see if I could get an internet connection. I like hearing French spoken. It's like wine to me. The tablet still wouldn't connect. Thank God I brought some books. They don't require recharging. Books are mysterious things. They have personalities. And psalms and truffles and storms and revelations. A spine. A table of contents. And lots of attitude.

Sometimes a book is big and sometimes it's small. Sometimes a book is hard to read and sometimes it's as simple as syrup. Sometimes it eats your brain and sometimes it walks around with a goblet making proclamations and spilling beer. Sometimes it's as elusive as intercourse and sometimes it's as loquacious as discourse. I don't know what to make of anything these days, much less literature, which was once a great distinction and is now threatened with extinction. I have an office to prosecute science. Fifty candles burn in my isolation. There's no hem to my indemnification nor residue to my syntax. The gears are so finely meshed they don't require generalities. And this all goes into a book. The book will obtain cash by reversing norms and grow into an autobiography of turmoil and opera. Queries in reference to scenery will be met with favorable regard. The answers will appear as trees. And forces in equilibrium, such as roses and gooseberry. Sometimes a book is a thousand volts and sometimes it folds itself into *omalumalu*. Hawaiian for "sheltering cloud." All the detours defeat the point of traffic lights and all the buffalo signal with their hands. The book is never-ending, which assumes for its premise an empire of infinite possibility. Quantum semantics. Radical acrobatics. Libraries of ice. Idealists swatting at gadflies. And to think the flute may have never existed. And that something that comes of nothing is a dwelling of smoldering obsessions, like *Lolita* or *Moby Dick*.

I liked our room. It was spacious and well-appointed with a huge bed and a bureau of drawers and two bedside lamps and a view of the ocean. The air conditioner was on when we first arrived and it was cold and felt like Seattle so I turned it off. When the room got hot I opened the sliding glass door and let the cool of the ocean air drift in and listened to the lulling rhythms of the surf. The elevator was strangely loud and got on my nerves. It seemed to run continuously between about five in the afternoon to eleven at night. One of the elevators was out of order. I guessed this added to the number of people riding it. But still. I wondered. Was there a line of people outside waiting for a free elevator ride? It made a hum and a whirr and a huff and a whine. I used some earplugs one night. There was a bed-side radio, but I could only find one station, pop music with those overproduced, digitized sounds that erode the music and fill it with ownership and gold. Jubilant eunuchs grinning at in-different sound engineers. Nothing honest or with real passion makes into the music scene these days. That's why I continually hear the old tunes at popular venues for booze and coffee and even grocery stores, The Beatles, The Rolling Stones, the Kinks, The Doors, The Shirelles, The Who, The Yardbirds. Sly and the Family Stone. Chuck Berry. Little Richard. Procul Harum. The Byrds. Led Zeppelin. Music over fifty years old. Weird.

Oriana got out her tablet and rested it on the bed covers and we tuned into the internet BBC 4 Extra programs, *The Goon Show* and *Reincarnathan* and *Ed Reardon's Week*. This was wonderful. It helped me sleep. Pot is still illegal in Hawaii and I missed my cannabis gummies and capsules. Silence and darkness aren't a good recipe for sleep. It forces me to pay attention to the circus in my head, the never-ending clown cars and weary elephants ridden by goblin ballerinas and near misses on the big top tra-peze. Remorse, guilt, despair, worries about the future. Then there's the whole issue of benign prostate enlargement. I have to get up a lot during the night to go to the bathroom. I frequently find myself wet with night-sweat. Anxiety isn't just an emotional state. It's my address. It was nice, on the way back to bed, to step out on the balcony and gaze at the stars. This affected me profoundly. It's a truism, but like a lot of truisms, it's true: when you gaze at the universe, you do begin to feel small and unimportant, and that epiphanous insight into my utter ephemerality and inconsequentiality helped put me asleep.

We went for a long run early in the morning, to avoid the heat, and then spent the rest of the day at leisure, sitting out on the balcony, reading and watching the surfers out on the ocean. I got out the binoculars to check out a tiny white thing fluttering in the breeze; it was a flag atop a buoy signaling that a diver was in the area. I also saw the faint mauve outline of what appeared to be a body of land to the west. This turned out to be Niihau, a small island whose population of eighty-four people are all Hawaiian natives. It was also home to Israel Kamakawiwo'ole, the Hawaiian musician best-known for his killer version of "Over the Rainbow," performed on the ukulele. This was the first time I discovered a body of land before seeing it on a map. It gave me a bit of a thrill.

We went for dinner at Lava's, but it was closed for a private function, so we crossed Poipu Road and went to Keoki's Paradise, a huge restaurant with a big tropical garden in its open center. Christmas music was playing and there were Christmas decorations everywhere. I found this jarring and strange since I was convinced this was summer. The staff were all quite nice and a talented musician performed on a stage in the garden area, mainly doing familiar pop songs, including "Over My Head," by Christine McVie, who had passed away a few days preceding.

On the way to Keoki's, I stopped to take a picture of the giant monkey pod tree in the orchid garden there. There appeared to be just enough light in the sky to get a coherent picture. The tree's branches ramified everywhere in curlicues of silly jubilant tree-joy. It looked octopal. And it broke my camera. I tried getting a picture of the fruit drink I ordered, and I heard it click, but when I went to review the picture, I couldn't access my other pictures, including the monkey pod tree. So I'm blaming the monkey pod tree. Or paradise. The sad thing about paradise is that it's always unobtainable, even when it's right in front of you. What makes paradise paradise is the ongoing, second-by-second wedding of earth and sky, and the absence of wealth, because nobody needs it. As Gonzalo puts it in *The Tempest*, all men idle, all, and women too, but innocent and pure; no sovereignty. One might also say it's subjective, that one person's paradise is another person's dystopia. Planet Earth was once a paradise. And then simians evolved and it all went to hell. Hell is other people, said Sartre. Just to make it clear. Honolulu isn't paradise.

Our flight home wasn't much better than the first, they were about the same in terms of discomfort, aggravation, frustration and despondency, except there were more babies. There was also a man I'd seen at the airport, big, fifty-something, just wearing shorts and a T-shirt, his arms and legs covered with deep red bruises and a few open sores, his arms raised, hands trembling. I wondered what in the world kind of disease this guy had. Could it be jellyfish stings? I felt bad for him. He really seemed to be suffering. I don't know where they put him on the plane — a special compartment in first class? — but I hope his six hours were more comfortable than mine.

I sat in the middle, Oriana by the window. My seatmate this time was an older gay man, retired, whose partner was across the aisle. He was affable, courteous, and a pleasant conversationalist. So there was at least that to be thankful for.

Once we were in the air, I dug *L'amour fou* out of my valise and hoped I could focus enough amid the din of crying children to escape into Breton's phosphorescent prose. It truly is magic.

It lifted me right out of my seat. My eyes lifted from the page and drifted upward to the soothing blue light in the overhead baggage compartments. Nice touch, that blue. So mellowing.

I come from a long tradition of poet maudits. We know we're shameless misanthropes, the Calibans of the human experiment. Restraint takes a lot of energy. But it keeps life civil.

I did get the stink-eye from a mother holding a baby. But I plead innocence. Blame it on a benign hypertrophic prostate. I would vastly have preferred to stay in my seat for the entire six-hour flight. Oriana somehow managed to pull that off. I was envious. I'm a mortal. And mortals need to slavishly satisfy the needs of the body. So off I went, maneuvering down the narrow aisle, marveling at the number of babies. Was I in a nursery? One of the three bathrooms was unoccupied. This is where things get tricky. I have to play therapist to my prostate to get it to relax and release its treasure, all while rocking back and forth in the tail of a jet airliner, leaning with my left shoulder on the wall to stabilize my body. I can see where someone might get impatient waiting to get into the bathroom. I'd get impatient. But come on, lady. I didn't choose to be old. Though maybe I did in some way. I did do everything favorable to the continuance of my existence. I guess you could call that a choice, an act of free will, or whatever free will one can muster in a web of contingencies. Nor did I choose to have a baby. You did, sister, that's on you.

In Seattle, everything changed, shifted back into cold, gray, dystopic stress. We went to the third floor of the parking garage to request a Lyft driver. Oriana found one right away, though we lost a few minutes trying to find him. It was bleak and confusing in the garage, all cold and concrete, people hurrying to catch their rides and get out of there. Get somewhere warm. A place to lie down. And stop pretending to be human. Because you're a mammal. And mammals need rest.

Molly was happy to see us. She couldn't get enough of our shoes. She kept sniffing them, trying to figure out where we'd been for so long. I don't know what conclusions she drew. But she shot around the apartment in joy.

I noticed a shift in attitude when we returned. My care about the world and what it did and didn't do and how the oceans were rising and species disappearing and war and famine worsening even as the richer nations grew increasingly indifferent to all the alarm bells going off was not as acute and full of rage as it had been. Had Kauai permeated me so deeply it turned my weltschmerz to wohlbefinden? No. Definitely not. I still had bile. Big as a tar pit. I could feel it bubble now and then. Dark wads of disdain rising into the miasmic night air and turning to phosphine balls of fire above the swamp. Foolish fire. Ignis Fatuus. I wasn't feeling lighter I was feeling more eroded. As if dying had begun. Which it had. Ever since I was born. It's everyone's dilemma. Here I am, life. For a brief while. This doesn't mean much in the beginning, it's just sophomoric pondering after a couple of beers. Death and decay, life and growth. That whole ying-yang thing. Cyclical paradoxes. Attachment is a better word. I was beginning to feel less attached. I'd go further and say I no longer felt like I belonged. This became all too apparent on our trip. Oriana did just about everything. I was lost. I don't understand the technology. I don't understand the zeitgeist. I don't understand people at all. I used to. Or thought I did. But equating free speech with hate speech? Liberals being all in support of censorship? To the point of pleading for it? The revelations of a journalist concerning atrocities and war crimes committed by the U.S. and its allies causing a minor fracas in the media and then jailed and tortured for years afterward while so-called journalists celebrated their profession at parties without a single mention of the journalist rotting in a British jail? WTF?!?

There's a part of you that feels good surrendering. Especially if there's a little extra sweetness added by an accompanying sense of futility. What may feel like struggle at first just ends up being the churn of emotion, an internal theater of adrenaline, norepinephrine and swamp gas. Imagine writing something so compelling, so stunning, so dynamic in its passion and commitment that it stirred a nation to heal itself and try to do better? End homelessness. End the wars. Exercise diplomacy. Stop profiteering from wars. That could work if people read. They've become illiterate. All they do is stare at their gadgets. Intellects rot. Brains atrophy. The next thing you know you're arguing over pronouns.

Add to this mix of satori and combustibility the disappearance of friends and family, even celebrities you've grown familiar with all your life and this will distance you even further from the coast, the country in which you were born. Its customs and timbre. Its timpani and fables. They fade. They disappear. Get put in museums. Will there be museums in the future? Libraries? Water fountains are gone. So, too, are payphones. Though I did see one in Kauai, on Lawai Road. A rooster was calling a chicken to ask why she crossed the road. To get to the other side you fucking moron, the chicken yelled. You see? Jokes like this belong in museums.

As people get dumber, the AI gets better. I often wonder what artificial intelligence is up to.

I also wonder if it wasn't language that brought us into the world. "Us" meaning creatures with tongues. And lips and teeth and uvula and palate. Which is a palette. A pallet of syllables. A forklift of ideas. Tread on a muddy road. Accommodations. Explosions. Syntax and glue.

Vocal cords aren't really chords they're folds of membranous tissue. They form a slit across the glottis whose edges vibrate in the stream of air to produce a cantata. Or an airplane.

Listen to the language at weddings. It goes through phases. It goes from stiltedness and anxious laughter to reverence and tears to vows and granite solemnity to champagne and cake and bad but enthusiastic dancing. A few people get lucky and a few get home just in time to vomit in the toilet.

Futility has been one of the more common roadside attractions of my life. I make frequent stops at futility stations. I fill my head with nihilism. Riot and confusion. Wait a minute. Incorrect. The world fills me with riot and confusion. The world is the Nile of my nihilism. Not the world world, the whirled world, the physical world, the planetary world, I mean the social milieu, the communal miasma, the social terrain, which can be described as illegible, and highly flammable. The external world and its expectations. The things that require your full attention. Things like cliffs. And sticky situations. And expensive lawyers. And bad constitutions. Disappearing constitutions. Constitutions eaten by greed. The mummies of congress, which are bloated and hungry, hungry ghosts, the kind that eat brains for breakfast and bribes for lunch. My level of participation in any of this has been minimal. Or at least that's what I'd like to think. I've spent an entire life believing reality was reality while knowing in reality reality was non-existent, it's a concept not an actuality. Looking at it all from a quantum, subatomic perspective. Which I do sometimes. But then when I see all those equations on a blackboard I have to wonder: is the sum of all butter better as a flavoring ingredient or as an emulsifying agent? If falling equals flying, then ship equals shape and the union of the onion is opinionable and pink, then rock equals roll and all things else will follow. Just be advised that I need to stop up ahead. I see a futility station.

What is it? I mean really, what is it? What are you hoping to get out of this? The second person is a dodge. I'm shifting perspective. Shifting blame. But I do mean you. This is sincere. This is a photogravure of the kieselguhr of candor. And I thank you. Thank you for being here.

Given the right tools and a good amount of time, I can make a placenta out of plywood, terabytes, knick-knacks, and quartz. But what would be the point if no one around here is pregnant? Are you pregnant? It's not mine. Whatever you say. I wasn't there. It wasn't me. I'm a scholar, not a scoundrel. But what is it? A boy or a girl? A scorpion or a bicycle wheel?

What's happening to me? I feel like a speedometer. Like I just got out of prison. Or was about to get out of prison. So which is it? Am I in prison? Or a prism? Prisms fragment light. I feel like a full spectrum has splintered apart. Life is happening to me. Out on the highway. The textures are slow. The scents are fast. The liniments are outstandingly understanding. Accelerations are elixirs. Combinations of things are axles and wheels and a chassis for the mind. I like velocity. I like things going in and out of me. I like going in and out of things. Are there gloves for this? Are there mirrors? The fountains have disappeared. They used to be everywhere. Bright little faucets ejaculating good public water into basins of sparkly socialism. That was before the billionaires scooped it all up and sold it back to everyone as a surveillance device.

It's amazing what you can do with a bunch of strings in your head. Travel assumes multiple forms. There are Tahitis of the mind, giant Polynesias of mystery and fruit. Paul Gaugin: "Where Do We Come From? What Are We? Where Are We Going." Strings are attached. Violin concertos. Son House. Robert Johnson. Lightnin' Hopkins. Sister Rosetta Thorpe. Altered and open tunings. Arpeggios, dropped D-tunings, inversions, picking, positions, power chords, tremolos and triads, octave pedals and pinch harmonics. These patterns will take you places, places you've never been, places where the rushes are plants instead of people, places where the pretzels are pretexts and epiphanies perpetual. Those occasions in which you can't tell inside from outside or outside from inside because all the dualities that've guided the wanderings of your mind have become a blur of distinctions whose fog eventually parts to reveal a body of land you've never seen before, or a detour that led to a strange dinner in a valley in Uganda. Or Mars. There's nothing on Mars, and yet I obsess over it, I'm into Martian porn, which is mainly all rocks and dust and a barrenness so stunning it fascinates even the dullest sensibility. It takes nine months to get to Mars. What you do there will have some bearing on your length of stay. I just want to strip my clothes off, wear a loincloth made from the hide of a leopard, and fly a pterodactyl around as I hunt for mummified proofreaders and psychedelic delicatessens.

Lightnin' Hopkins stayed with a basic three chord (tonic, subdominant, dominant) guitar pattern to go with his vocal phrasing, which didn't always match the metrics of the music, which is what I like about it, that vital discordance that brings it alive.

When Jaz Coleman sings "I Am the Virus" it reminds me of Lennon's "I Am the Walrus," both songs subversive in their own way, Lennon's goofy surrealism undermining the assumed supremacy of logic and reason in the Western cultures, Coleman's rage, which has been distilled into liquid white lightning, easily as contagious as any microbe, the virus in question being the virus of art, virus of language, virus of antinomianism, virus of insurgency and outcry.

The Killing Joke song preceded Covid by about five years. Weird.

Fiction is a delicate thing. It's the membrane between the actual and the peripheral. Gypsies with a white Percheron pulling a red wagon on a yellow day on a blue planet. That could be either fiction or an ovulation of helter-skelter kingdoms in a single testament. The truth is never simple. It's generally convoluted. Like lettuce, or cabbage. Nothing normal is ever prudent. It doesn't have to be. It's the aberrant that renders our irritations to the piling under the Santa Monica boardwalk. Things have to be worked out. Puzzled through. Pieces joined. Words aligned. I'm over my head, but it sure feels nice. Fiction is pharmacology, the truth is piracy. It comes swinging toward you with a look of mania and a knife in its teeth. Fight back. Tell a lie. It won't stop the truth. But it's morning and there isn't a jury around for miles. You can say what you want. Here's the problem: the universe doesn't conform to our language. And so when something like the truth comes around, it's generally unadorned, and unencumbered by law.

Did you know Chekhov's body was transported to Moscow in a refrigerated railway car meant for oysters? A little ironic, yes, but also a little pragmatic, really. A good pair of skis should be your first priority. A disinterested perspective should be your second. Things like clothes, hair, accessories, warm water, pretty sounds, and Thich Nhat Hanh. Dancing is an odd thing to do. I think it proves something. Something like Florida. My point being: the elbow is in control of its own reality. You don't need to change a thing. But tell me: why is pain necessary? This is what life does when death isn't around. It cares for things and tries not to kill anyone. Consciousness is the ghost of an exuberance. I'd keep it under my hat if I were you. The zeitgeist needs a bath.

Metaphysical nihilism cannot negate the impulse toward understanding. This is how life gives itself to us: in warm water, getting abundant sunlight. A lot of conflict emerges from the discrepancy that we have of our feelings and the material reality which temporarily gives them birth, said Lucretius. Well, yeah, I'd say that's one way to get attention. Another might be wearing clogs. Blowing soap bubbles for a cheetah. Masturbation in a grocery cart. Do thoughts have substance? In a word, no. But incandescence doesn't go well with small talk and Wheat Thins. Intensity is easily mistaken for Caravaggio. Consciousness always has a good reason to write itself down. My first instinct in all things is to grip something and hang on for dear life. Now do you believe me? No? Good. Grab that idea and run with it. Score a point for the inexplicable.

I have faith in immanentism. It lies on the floor in a miasma of eggs and syntax. Well-being has a way of murmuring its nonchalance to whatever train happens to be moving through the wilderness. Everything else retires into fingers. Stars ooze punctuation on the South China Sea. We rest below deck balancing the scent of union labor with the stench of creosote. There was a time when one could wander the aisles of a hardware store and find things that mattered. Nuts and bolts. Shovels and ventriloquists. Miniskirts and vocabulary. The seagulls gathered at a point in the sky and then began boiling if the words mattered. Intuitions suggest walking. The fog bends itself into toes. Pyramids have a point. This is a messy place. The houses are full of failure, which makes them noisy. You can feel it in the arms. The logic of catastrophe, which is words.

Consciousness means we're involved in the creation of the universe. It's a process. What you're going to need is a philosophy, a shovel, and a bag of cement. Romance, precision, generalization. Quills and calculus and pliers and a caulking gun and motorcycles and a big garage. A drummer. A bass guitarist. A case of beer. The voice of Merle Haggard. The spirit of Moses. The linguistic prowess of Cleopatra. A stiff felt hat and a whirlpool of upholstery in somebody's basement. Lights are good and a Persian carpet and a roll of duct tape. Include a peninsula and a noontime snooze. Everyone is here. Everyone is involved. It's time to get started. This one's all but gone. But we can salvage the nails and lumber. It's going to be a kick-ass universe. Timeless as string. If we do it up right, it will echo the cravings of the spirit. And walk in beauty like the yo-yo.

I'm a yo-yo. No doubt about it. It amazes me the number of times I have to get up and piss. The night becomes a pattern of up and down, up and down, up and down. Pissing has become an occupation. I've had to cultivate a new relationship with my body and its organs. In youth I flew around like Ariel, hardly aware I had a body at all. Unless I had a hard-on. Or I was getting punched in a fight. Because some guy's girlfriend took a liking to me. And gave me a hard-on. But sometime after passing fifty things changed. And by the time I was seventy I became the caretaker of 170 pounds of elements like hydrogen and sulfur and phosphorous and an amalgam of muscle, gum and bone. I do what it wants. What it needs. And now if you'll excuse me, I have to piss.

Remember when people used to say stupid things like job satisfaction is a cause of well-being? They don't still say that, do they?

I'd rather shoot myself. I hope to God I never become that person. Which, considering my age, is highly unlikely. I'm a different species of asshole. I'm the kind that goofs off all day, ruminating on the treacheries and hazards of the world, too busy spinning a little hamster wheel in my brain to take arms against a sea of troubles, rehashing old dialogues, arguments with people long dead, the calamities of life, Whips and Scorns of Time, then blames it all on Arthur Schopenhauer.

The spawn of John Calvin is everywhere. Original sin. Predestination. Humility and obedience. Hard work as a religious duty. Jesus. What bullshit.

Those forced grins you used to see everywhere, at least that's gone. Now that the corporate juggernaut has achieved its goal of hijacking governments and prosecuting a plan of neo-feudalism for the masses, it's ok to show your despair and look askance and not engage customers in conversation. Those self-serve aisles at the grocery store have become a remarkable success. It's got work, martyrdom, and debasement all over it and as an added bonus you don't have to engage with anyone.

Whatever happened to well-being? For a lot of people, people fleeing Afghanistan or Ukraine or Syria, it's a luxury. It begins with shelter and food. And for a lot of people — many of them living in the United States and Europe — shelter and food have become a luxury.

There's no such thing as well-being. Being is a meaningless term. It's not an entity. Not a cotton swab. And what does "well" mean?

Skilled, competent, good, healthy, strong, vigorous, shrewd, judicious, fit as a fiddle. In other words, an asshole. Non-being is a form of well-being. If there's no being, there's no worry, no purpose, no agenda, no target, no intention, no weaponry, no animus, no machinations, no aim. Therefore, non-being is the halo of a long reverie. Blue rubies. Black Beauties. Musical breweries. I'm done now. Done with being. This is clearly the moment to talk about something else. Eccentrics in Tibet and the rhetoric of flapping shirts. Cherry blossom pink is the nipples's buddy, and this is a reference to paint, to a full understanding of form, and the emptiness of form, and nothingness of hue on the tip of a camelhair brush.

It's a simple formula: if you have non-being, nobody can get their hooks in you. When well-being becomes a commodity, non-being is a way out: ownership is suffering. When you ain't got nothing, you got nothing to lose.

Normally, I don't get this preachy. But every time I see a white blank sheet of paper or white glaring block of word document I see a theater. I see a stage. I see Richard Burbage. And Shakespeare. So here I am. To be or not to be, that is the question. Everything pivots around that.

I try watching Elvis Presley on YouTube do his special in 1968 and sing "That's All Right" with gusto. But I get a cramp in my foot. Normally I stand on my foot until the muscle loosens and flattens out and my anatomy goes back to looking recognizably human. But I rode it out. It's the first time I'd seen him do that since I first saw it on TV in 1968. He puzzled me then. He maintained that look. The hair swept back with a pompadour spilling smartly over his brow. Black leather shirt, black leather pants. That really dangerous look. The hippies jettisoned that look for the more eccentric apparel of the sacred fool. The Beats didn't really have a look. Plaid shirts and jeans, maybe. Working class. Lumberjacks. Merchant seamen. Dishwashers. Drunken Buddhists. Moppers. Brooders. Bodhisattvas. But that's all right now mama, anyway you do.

8:13 P.M. Monday night. December. Cold and dark. A violinist plays Vivaldi's "Violin Concerto in A Minor" on YouTube. I fall asleep. I wake up. Good thing the laptop didn't fall on the floor. Got to watch that in the future. Nodding off is so easy these days. Happens a lot. Just as I sink into oblivion I pass through a funny phase of half-consciousness in which strange, irrational scenarios unfold. I believe the term for this is hypnagogia. I can never retrieve them in time. They dissipate faster than kitchen steam. It's rare if they leave a clue behind. It's a little frustrating. I don't know what to call these reveries. They are, of course, reveries, but reveries of a very specific kind. They're as delinquent in logic as they are delicate in duration.

There is one that persists, an image that developed a permanency in my brain after staring at it for four days, which was the horizon on the Pacific from our hotel in Poipu Beach, Kauai. It was so utterly infinite, and empty. I didn't see a single ship. No whales. No giant reptilian creature rising from the deep, grabbing a luxury catamaran and eating it like a sandwich, as the passengers drop into the ocean like slices of raw onion. The vastness needed some spice, which I was glad to provide, imposing my mind on it like a stencil over a textured surface.

Earlier today Oriana told me a married couple in their sixties were snorkeling about fifty yards off-shore at Keawakapu Point in south Maui just before noon last Thursday. The husband saw a shark swim by several times and suddenly his wife was nowhere to be found. The man returned to shore and reported his wife missing. Rescuers searched the area for three days before calling off the search after a twelve-foot-long tiger shark had been spotted. I wondered about sharks when we were in Kauai and contemplated going for a swim. Even taking surfing lessons. I tried it once many years ago in Santa Cruz, California. It's a difficult sport. Windsurfing is even harder. I remember spending several hours in a small lake near my brother's house while he tried teaching me how to windsurf. He had a passion for windsurfing and was quite good at it. I could barely stand upright on the board.

I can spend hours surfing the internet as one idea opens another idea which leads inevitably to another idea into something like a non-linear collage of songs and species of fish and gemstones and medieval weaponry floating around randomly in my brain. But if you look toward the bottom, down in the sand and partially buried is a treasure chest of fears, phobias, obsessions and shiny ingots of epiphanic gold. High on my hierarchy of fears is that of being eaten by a shark. I got anxiety from looking far out on the waves to see surfers waiting for a swell, legs dangling in the water. I can only imagine how tantalizing that must be to a shark who hasn't eaten for days. I expressed as much in conversation with a friend who is a filmmaker living in North Carolina. He's doing a movie about a poet who worked many years as a deep-sea diver and then lost his certification when he insisted he got gonorrhea from a siren. It's going to be called *Unfathomable* and will star Nicolas Cage as the poet, celebrated author of a book of poetry called *Rapture of the Deep*, with the poems "Tango With a Tiger Shark," "Octopus's Garden Redux," "Bottom Time," "Buddy Breathing" and "I Fell Deep in Love and Got the Bends."

I love the sound of Lucinda William's voice it takes me right out to the prairie and open spaces and all the cruel and beautiful things that happen under those skies. The way she sings Dylan's "Tryin' to Get to Heaven Before They Close the Door" opens you to all its mysteries and staggering beauty, riding the treacherous waters of the Mississippi or smelling clods of rich dark dirt upturned by a moldboard plow. Rural. Yes. But the richness of all that and the sadness and fortitude and the furrows of sound a strong voice makes in the air. It's a seasoned voice. The front of it is warm and fundamental and the trailing edge is foreboding as distant thunder.

I go feed the cat and eat some raisins out of the bag with a teaspoon. I wish they wouldn't put raisins in bags. I like the canisters. They stay put until you come to collect them. But with a bag they're harder to control. They spring to the side and drop to the floor or shoot behind the breadboard. The kitchen is full of adventures.

Oriana is sitting at her table with her mini-Kauai to the right, lower down on a small table, two fuchsias and a Christmas cactus lapping up light in furious growth, watching Peter Sellers in a TV interview that aired back in the 1970s, judging by the haircuts of Sellers and the TV host, long and spilling over the ears, but impeccably groomed. Oriana has become an avid *Goon Show* fan. I return to the bedroom and hear bursts of laughter.

Randy Meisner comes on singing "Take It to the Limit." There so much yearning and melodic resignation in his voice, deeply sad, fraught with uncertainty, but yearning, craving intensity for the sake of intensity, the song of the open road, appeasing one's woes and lostness with the velocities of the highway night. His voice soars into the arena like a strong beam of light.

Here I am at seventy-five still thinking I have things to achieve. It's funny. What can I achieve in a handful of years? I won't be getting a law degree. I won't be going to med school. I won't be joining the Marines. I won't be going to a police academy. But maybe I can invent something. Maybe I can write a dissertation on the beautiful insufficiency of the little toe and what that means in terms of screwing a lightbulb into a lamp or listening to Stevie Ray Vaughan.

It has long been my destiny to say silly things to silly people. And have I exhausted everything concerning the sound of castanets in a television studio and the sweet fall of rain in Puerto Rico?

Bungee-jumping was never on my bucket list. I'm not particularly drawn to the zip-line experience either. I want to sit in a bar in a small Midwestern town drinking whisky and listening to the jukebox. Maybe Marcel Duchamp will come in and show me his latest readymades, a pair of oven mitts and a Smith and Wesson .38 revolver. He looks good in a ten-gallon hat. He collects dust and puts it on a sheet of glass and shoots it and calls it a revelator.

I haven't had an actual drink in years. I fantasize about drinking. It's difficult, because I can't quite remember what it was like to be drunk. I do remember the hangovers. I wish there were a way to reverse that. Remember the drunks and forget the hangovers. But then I'd end up drunk. With a terrible hangover the next day.

Oriana tells me about a female poet who lives in the desert who sees a lot of crows and vultures. Crows I know. I get mobbed by crows when I step outside and go for a walk. I know next to nothing about vultures. Except that they feed on the dead and look prehistoric. If turkeys became funeral directors, they'd look like vultures. Which are amazing birds. They can smell carrion from over a mile away. Their bald head helps them stay clean when feeding on a carcass. They help keep nature clean. Nature has a tendency to get dirty. Even dirt gets dirty occasionally, contaminated with sewage, oil, arsenic, and lead. Vultures fly on thermals, an upward current of air. As did my father. He loved flying gliders. I went up with him a few times. Once when I was hungover. I got nauseous and he got me back to the ground with astonishing speed. He was an amazing flyer. I'd help, occasionally, to retrieve his plane if he came down hundreds of miles from the airfield. Eagles would often circle with him as he rode a thermal. He never mentioned vultures. Vultures are equipped with a digestive system that employs special acids to dissolve anthrax, botulism, and cholera bacteria. Vultures practice urohidrosis, defecating on the scaly parts of their legs to cool them by evaporation. If I ever run a marathon in a hot climate, I might give it a try. But how would I achieve that? I don't quite understand the mechanics of it. I'd have to use my hands. Yuk. Vultures vomit as a tactical maneuver against adversaries. That I can do. Egyptian vultures use rocks to break open ostrich eggs. Another bird I know very little about. Between 1999 and 2005, nearly a hundred griffon vultures were released into France's Verdon gorge near Rougon, a small village in southeast France. Eleven monk vultures were released in that region in 2005. Also visible in the Verdon gorge are golden eagles, peregrine falcons, and the red-billed chough. How many Westerns have I seen in which vultures are spotted in the distance, filling the screen with the grim reality of death, and the graceful circling of vultures?

I love Westerns. That genre of movie seems to be disappearing. Wonder why. What is it about Westerns? The wild west and its mythology of gunslingers and cardsharps holds a constant fascination for me. I remember that incident in Mark Twain's *Roughing It* where he keeps getting thunked in the back of the head by a dictionary flying around on the Overland Stage he and his brother, Orion Clemens, rode from St. Joseph, Missouri, to Carson City, Nevada, after Orion had been appointed secretary of Nevada Territory. I remember on a road trip through Nevada in the late 1980s seeing the remnants of a stagecoach station and wondered if it might've been the one Twain described. I remember gazing at the sky while crossing an alkaline desert and how alien and vast everything seemed, and a sign in the desert which I initially took to be a Sinclair Oil gas station sign, which depicted a long-necked dinosaur, brontosaurus, if memory serves, but turned out to be a sign for a whorehouse, a woman in fishnet stockings and stiletto heels, with one of the associates outside in a T-shirt and pair of shorts washing the windows.

And what was it — after all these years — did I expect to get out of life? Every time I avert my eyes to the right I get a taste of Nice: a print of a woman standing nude on a red carpet holding a towel with the hint of a palm tree in a window. She's calm and relaxed and expressionless, adrift in an indefinable moment. Adjectives are radical. Anything that happens in life can be seasoned with a few adjectives and jacked up into exceptional ruminations that break the monotony with the force of their conviction. Memories exist to heave forward with everyone laughing. Otherwise they're just memories, the kind of creaky vinyl that upholsters the quieter places in the mind where confessions happen, and French fries and straws. I can't explain the behavior of this language, or how it got here, but I feel the weight of it struggling to make sense of salsa.

I like to maneuver independently of confusion. It helps with my sewing. There's nothing under my control. Never has been. It's why I'm such a sucker for pronouns. I have grounds to dismiss the monuments. They can go home now. Home to the grandeur of despair and the chop of helicopters. Everything is fights and prostitution. I renounced my life as a gunslinger and coaxed sleep into accepting me. Chris Stapleton sang at our wedding. The marriage of heaven and hell. The genesis of meanings. The tears of fish nailed to the beams of heaven. Cézanne thumped his chest and painted a plate of fruit and chanterelle. I stood there and cried as hallucinations poured out of my eyes. Derelict black clouds, sexual deviancy and Richard Burton walking on broken glass. Is this life? Or just a sophomoric romp in the barn? If you take a look around you, what you see is cows and straw. Nothing more than a metaphor, really, dizzying and agricultural.

It's been snowing all night. Surely, in the morning, there'll be something to see. The world and its details homogenized in white. The light we see right now is two and half million years old, and could use a shower. Sometimes, in the darkness, I can feel my chains loosen. I can hear foghorns and trains. With the right set of tools, pain can be negotiated. Mindfulness meditation works for some. I get little out of it, but some people swear by it. I like cannabidiol. You can feel it in the body. A warm diffusion of well-being that loosens knots and idles the engines of worry.

What did I do today? Oh brother, lots of things. Rolled around in thread. Sparkled like an urge. Howled at a meditation. Chiseled an allegory out of a box of candy. Communed with the hum of the refrigerator. Rushed into myself with an orthogonal lake and a Cubist forklift. Made an athletic sandwich with a slice of life and a jar of uplifting failure. Exceeded my expectations by kissing a complete stranger. Emptied a pharmaceutical joke. Scrubbed the flickering babble of a heavy demand. Baked a pocket in denim. Conquered a noodle. Watched the emphasis. Changed my mind. Unraveled a wrinkled architecture. Thwacked an escalator with heaven. Drew a conclusion from my underwear drawer. Painted an emotion. Cooked a book. Considered the lilies. Grew a ponytail. Built a wrinkle. Invented a disease. Flashed like a road sign. Burped.

It's easy to fuck. Nobody gets hurt by fucking but madmen and madwomen. Is that true? My hunger creates a food that everybody needs.

Remarked Bernadette Mayer on page 111 of *Proper Name*. Wonderful poet, Bernadette Mayer. She passed away November 22nd, 2022, less than a month ago. Oriana and I just found out about it yesterday. Oriana and I had a deep appreciation of her work, which was always full of energy and spontaneity and keen observations about daily life. We also greatly admired her devotion to the art of poetry, which entailed years of poverty, which she embraced with grace and fortitude.

Funny word, fortitude. Courage in pain or adversity. Adversity plays rough. I don't like it. But I agree with the Duke in Shakespeare's *As You Like It*: "Sweet are the uses of adversity, / Which, like the toad, ugly and venomous, / Wears yet a precious jewel in his head. / And this our life, exempt from public haunt, / Finds tongues in trees, books in the running brooks, / Sermons in stones, and good in everything. / I would not change it." Amen, brother.

Adversity thrives in Seattle. The homeless encampments keep getting bigger. The one down on Roy Street near Lake Union, cattycorner to the Paul Allen Institute, keeps growing, though in late summer it seemed to explode into chaos and several of the tents went missing a day or two later. We remember seeing a man — half naked with a wild bush of hair — standing in the middle of Ninth Avenue North — an extremely busy street — gesticulating and shouting imprecations at a horde of invisible demons. Invisible to us, maybe not to him. He was like King Lear. He eyed us and we picked up our pace. I'm not prepared just yet to play Mad Tom to his King Lear.

Sweet are the uses of adversity. Can't say I'm 100% on board with that. For starters, I don't have a jewel in my head. But I do like to think of myself as a toad. A Sonoran desert toad, to be precise. If you tickle my glands, I will secrete 5-methoxy-N,N-dimethyltryptamine, a potent psychedelic of the tryptamine class. So I retract my statement: I do have a jewel in my head.

This afternoon I transferred the pictures I took in Kauai from my digital camera to my laptop. I got about three good ones. The rest were lousy. The chain link fence in the two shots I got of the water spraying out of a hole at Spouting Horn Park and several tourists — also taking pictures — spoiled the potential either might've had for impact. The one I took of Roberta on the balcony with the Pacific Ocean in the background wasn't bad, but it was too dark. She was too much in shadow. The best ones were a shot of the sunset which was quite beautiful — the clouds — wispy and wonderfully ethereal — were imbued with contrasting colors of pink and violet and gold. Two palm trees stand out sharply, giving the shot its quintessential stamp of equatorial tropicality.

It's an iconic photograph — as exemplary of a tropical paradise in a crepuscular setting as any drugstore postcard — with more than a hint of bourgeois hedonism about it — but I like it. It's not unique. Nothing at all unique about it. But the colors are imbued with a sense of the marvelous (I do like to persuade myself that I caught the sky at a particular moment of insane beauty that was out of the ordinary, touched with the supernatural, with a savage holiness), and I never imagined I'd be in a place like that, a tiny speck in the North Pacific overrun with wild chickens. Our being there was something of a fluke, it being Oriana's retirement gift. Never thought I'd see Hawaii. It wasn't high on my bucket list. Not out of disinterest, I just never thought I'd have reason to go there. And I didn't. The only reason we chose Kauai over, say, Omaha, Nebraska, or Phoenix, Arizona (we couldn't agree on San Diego), was curiosity. What's it like to be in a warm climate away from harsh wet Seattle winter? And now we know: it's fucking wonderful.

The fact this one particular photograph is a sunset and not a dawn is significant to me. I'm old. Seventy-five as of this writing. I'm in the twilight phase of my life. The day and its pleasures and tribulations have come to an end and the night is seeping into the air like a cool black liquid of stars and oblivion. The day is lemonade. The night is wine. Of course, when the sun is going down on your side of the horizon it's dawn on the other side. Night in Kauai. Dawn in Taiwan.

Nor did I break my camera on the monkey pod tree. That picture came out great. The branches shout out like dendrites in a cosmic brain.

The most persistent image was not a photograph but an image in my mind. It occurred the moment I put Bréton's *L'amour fou* down and took a peek out of the window. Oriana was immersed in Melville's *Omoo*, so I had a clear shot. I'd been doing that every minute or so. I was anxious to see land. Desperate to see land. I couldn't wait to get off the plane. And there it was: a discernible mass of land coming out of the mist. My sense of relief was acute. That's what photographs don't do. They don't capture the flavor of the moment, the gestalt, the sensorium, the way a chair feels, the way the air smells, the noises going on around you, the imponderable, the unquantifiable, the descent through thick equatorial mist and that sharp bump when the wheels hit the tarmac. The roar of the engines slowing the plane's thrust. The quiet as everyone suspends their conversation. The taxi to the airbridge. Yanking our suitcase from the overhead compartment. Saying goodbye to the crew. The pilots always look so happy and congenial. Then that initial surprise, warm air. That's when that feeling comes, that you've just entered a dream.

I've never been much of a photographer. My flirtations with it haven't produced much of anything except frustration and dis-appointment. Cameras are fussy. They always manage to break when I get my hands on them. The digital camera is virtually fool-proof. But not for this fool. Who took it on a journey and broke it on a monkey pod tree.

Was it the manifest cosmic energy of this tree that broke my camera, or am I mythologizing a body of botanical life because it suited what I was feeling — or attempting to feel — at that moment? I do incline toward the theatrical. Even in old age. I'm old. My camera is old. Anything electronic these days is consid-ered old once it exceeds five years of use. And — to be honest — my camera wasn't entirely broken. It was behaving differently, but it wasn't defunct. Was it the tree? Or my proclivity toward the fantastical? I'd make a terrible camera. I do believe in a higher reality. The sublime. The miraculous. The imaginative. Pragma-tism is an insult to my nervous system. The empirical is a trampoline to get bounced into the ether of fantasy. I can, however, get carried away. Hyperbole can lead to artifice. Extravagance is great. But it can also suffocate.

All too often these escapades into the preposterous and over-wrought are due more to the exuberance of words than a desire to grandstand like a circus announcer. I like it when that happens. It's a funny thing, interposing a medium between the actuality of our being and what we're thinking and feeling and the external world. Distortions are inevitable. One might as well enjoy them.

It can be a real tricky maneuver to get a body of words to do what you want them to do. Languages have lives of their own. Emotions are by nature messy and resist intrusions from the abstract. The radius of the unreal hovers high over the cacophony of day-to-day calculus in a backwoods kitchen. The brood of tools in a basement closet. The quarry of query in a block of marble. The flex of an open dress. The embassy of reason in an empire of the mad. This is what words do when they're not corralled properly. They stampede. They break loose. They scatter into the hills. I can't describe these hills because the words ran off and disappeared into them. I wonder what they're doing. Ruminating, chewing grass, would be my speculation. These are the words that stayed. They chew like ungulates in ruminant stillness, and make splendid scenery.

"Like bodies, language produces and reproduces itself; in each syllable lies a seed (*bija*) that, on being actualized in sound, is a vibration emitting a form and a meaning."
—Octavio Paz, "Blank Thought"

It's hard dragging an emotion into a paragraph. If the emotion doesn't know why it's being drug into a paragraph, the emotion is reluctant to go. Emotions like being expressed, and writing is of particular appeal because emotions are sloppy, amorphous energies of fog and hysteria, and they like the crisp alertness of letters and words that strongly convey a flair for definition, that's a huge snorkel party for any emotion, but they don't want to be put on display for no reason, it's embarrassing, like Cary Grant knitting socks in a store window in the 1943 movie *Mr. Lucky*. Once it has been well-established that this is a paragraph being assembled for the express purpose of showcasing the emotion and itemizing its grudges and hopes and disappointments and aspirations, it's time to bring out the ground crew and Muddy Waters and get some mojo going.

Complex phenomena can be described with a few fundamental principles. But not everything. The incalculable is truly incalculable. I prefer reading. I've got enough books to stack all the way to the sky, where there's folklore and lightning. The sky, of course, is huge and ludicrous, just like language, which structures and determines our apprehension of reality, that very thing I went in search of years ago only to find Peter Green sitting on a rock with a piece of cheese in his hair. Death is a private affair. It's an occupational hazard, like enzymes and sleeves. You can take it with a grain of salt. But one day the sky will speak to you in a very soft voice, and ask you if you're ready. Ready to do what? Not do, be. Ready to feel the sun under your skin. Ready to let go. And walk into heaven with a smile. A rhythmical flow. And a piece of cheese in your hair.

What's the difference between a theory and a chair? A chair is everything and a theory is fungus. Be careful which mushrooms you choose to put in the sauce. Here's what to look out for: money becoming a deity. When that happens, no one has intelligence and the sublime gets buried in bullshit. You see New Age

Silicon Valley billionaires dining on steak and lobster at Burning Man and tent cities in all the parks. It takes a lot of words to say nothing. Tanning salons impel reflection. If the universe is matter and energy, might there also be some sourdough? You're thinking: who is this asshole? I will tell you: I'm a book bewildering as a tumor. Morality doesn't exist in nature. But grace and energy do. Take a look at the highway. This is where words hobnob with introspection. Theories don't cure ignorance. But at least they don't create it.

I often wonder what a stick could do if I stuck it in some twine. If you look fast, you'll see the answer recoiling into the night. I'm clearly not in control here. Something happened in paradise. Something huge and irresistible. Calling things into question. Floating the beautiful immodesty of diamonds. Meaning is the glue holding abstractions together in their cerebral acrobatics. Spirit rippling ocean sand. A diver plunging into a wave. A worry buttressed against the void. An image is to thought what words are to nerves. They swarm the attic with the frenzy of inference. Folds of old linen. The sway of beach grass when the wind is from the east. The scent of kind letters comforts the discerning when the wind is from the west. When the wind is from the south we lie on a bed and open a can of cricket crimes. And when the wind is from the north the wall undertakes a mass of prisms and breaks the sun into a million shards of heat and gold. A carpenter slides down the embankment to the shore. Each reverie is a nail pounded into the hull of a giant chartreuse. The writing body grows feathers. Takes wing. And disappears.

I always knew it. That I would end up like this. That I would find myself here. What was my contribution? What were my omissions? What did I bring to this current dystopia? What will come after us? After the final bomb. The final bullet. The final asphyxiation. What fossils? Will the bones of humans be reassembled in museums many eons in the future? I doubt there'll be a planet. It'll be swallowed by the sun. Which will be a red giant. Swallowing its children. As did the corporate entities that made life impossible. Museums are a singularly human invention. Sponsored by corporations. First they kill things. And then they build museums. Here's an idea. Don't kill things. Don't build museums. But if there must be a museum, let it be a museum of musing. Musing was once a distinction. Musing could use a museum. An amusing museum. Nothing in it but musing. Skeins of brain in lavish crisis. Unraveling in the bliss of eschewal.

Welcome to the chestnut socialite club. There's a worm dreaming of thin things and pink things and palpable things in the accommodation of its dirt. Such tinctures rinse the panorama of pain and bring clarity to a sink. Tears furrow the face. The attic grows a pair of hands. This species of phenomenon is known by its climate, which is thick and indecipherable, like Medicare. I feel a change pulsing in all these little decals. I've never been a stickler for rawhide. But if you're going anywhere near the saloon tonight, I'd think about a black tie and a crawling kingsnake around your naked torso. Plus a badge. A big shiny one. Pinned to your chest like a surge of solicitude. Maturity, after all, has an ocher disposition, and propagates by trigonometry in the summer, when the circles are banging, and the mailboxes are hives of symptomatic effusion.

I agree. I don't deny it. All in all, this is very cutesy, very thin and very unmanly. Art for art's sake. Really? Yes, really. When art is burdened with a political agenda it ceases to be art. It becomes a tank, flattening one and all with its monotonous tread. But isn't art for arts's sake a political stance? Yes, it is. But a very sexy one.

With a .38 special tucked in a pocket holster. And a samurai sword hidden in a pink flamingo bathrobe. For those hungover mornings. When the gunfire is intermittent and loud. And the piano is being used for firewood. And there's still some faith in the transmundane. This is a messy place. You can feel it in the shoulder. The blossoming of a lotus. And this is called art for art's sake. So for goodness' sake. Put it by the window and give it some water. Some attention. And let it do nothing. But remind us of beauty.

There can be, then, purposiveness without purpose, so far as we do not place the causes of this form in a will, but yet can only make the explanation of its possibility intelligible to ourselves by deriving it from a will. Said Immanuel Kant. I'm not ready to make a religion of it, but I get what he intends. It has purpose. It's like a magnetic hook in a garden of words. The determining ground of its cause precedes it with a hot iron. Let's get the wrinkles out. Wrinkles serve no purpose. This makes them perfect for discourse. Or intercourse. It's your game. But it's my iron. Sometimes I feel like I'm falling into a life I didn't intend. But I'm not going to bicker with my knees in this chasm. Immoderate combing leads to pills. Oblongs and hearts. Like the hive at Butter Lake. You can skip the slides. Water has never been an annoyance. Except for that one time the Pacific tried to pull me out of this world. Everything sparkled. How do you do it? How do you capture a mood? You just do. You wrestle it into a cage. And then release it into the wild.

Muscles stir unions. I sleep in a skull of Capernaum. The houses are full of swooning melody, and arguments and snoring. Stars are thoughtless, magic rags of nonchalance. Some seagulls occurred to me just now. I like them. But I prefer the gliding of swans. If the words are boiling, you might consider the cravings of the spirit. Try meditating during sports events. If a football falls on your lap, you can trade it in for a shovel and comb your hair. People can tell you what happened later. I have no idea what Nietzsche means when he says that morality has a sensual squirt. I think it's more like the thorny tongue of a flight attendant. Metaphysical nihilism cannot negate the impulse toward understanding. But it can get in the way of making pretty sounds. Do thoughts have substance? No. But they do have fire escapes and alleys. And sound like pigeons.

In physiology, tonotopy is the spatial arrangement of where sounds of different frequency are processed in the brain. In poetry, tones close to each other in terms of frequency are floated to the top of an abandoned warehouse after pollinating a poem by Mallarmé. This is how the poem makes its food. You may wonder what it takes to roast a noun in the flames of poetry. The root must be long and languorous as spine water in a lawn pillow. It's only then that the tigers of the West visit us in the night with their phantom sounds and spiritual needs. Recently, a theoretical multiphase compensation mechanism at a cortical level appeared to me with a poem that had initially been hypothesized as a song by John Fogarty, who is still active and auditory as ever. I put a spell on you because you're mine. Do you see how delusional and desperate things can get down here? Beam me up, Scotty! I don't know. It's crazy. I'm old enough to get high on anything. Just a smile makes me giddy. The universe slides up and down in my blue jelly pants. And every morning the rumble of Mallarmé's Harley excites the bees at the border of the real.

It's snowing tonight. This is fitting, since we have fingers and hands. We're also five days out from Christmas. Which was once a feeling. And now it's a juggernaut. Even though the malls are gone. And the streets are crowded with UPS, Fed Ex and Amazon Prime trucks. We still drink it in. Still spend money on it. Still hang wreathes on the door. We use symbols to communicate with one another. Baubles, lights, lobsters, glass, gloss, glaze, dog-eared books and mongrel emojis. Chameleons climb the walls looking for the tropics. The kitchen sink is popular with wasps. I go dancing in my memory. That day I saw John Lennon walking down the street and muttered hello. I have high hopes for the purposeless balm of the writing I'm sometimes doing. You can create anything with words. But it's not entirely scrupulous. Remember to land your face somewhere gentle. Let the ground accept your weight. You can do anything if you put your mind to it. Bury your head in snow. Try pushing it with your mind. It'll melt before you reach the next metaphor. I'm glad we got in the car and got some cannabis gummies. We probably won't be able to drive tomorrow. The snow keeps coming. My mind keeps trying to push it. Push it with words. Big ones, made of metal, and grit, and the black silver of ice in the dead of night.

There are those days you wake up and have some coffee and you want to consume everything, as much experience as possible, read as many books as possible, because books are possibility on paper, possibility with a spine, possibility undercover, possibility in a texture, in a canoe, in an engine of words, which is a poem, which is a set of peculiarities, eccentricities circling a testimony, a witnessing, and a walk in the park, which is icy today, the crunch and crackle of ice underfoot. And this is called experience. And is a mountain to climb. It develops a dish. An engorged sense of life which may be served to people on a platter of morning. And is gold. And calls attention to itself. Scrambled eggs and bacon. Warm muffin. First word to form in the mouth.

If, for example, you needed a mustache, and you couldn't grow one, would you nail one to your mouth? I recommend mahogany. In all things. Not just as a prosthesis for facial hair. It makes a good coffin as well. Or a guitar. They say protons give an atom its identity, electrons its personality. I say poetry gives the provocateur a bomb, metaphors its explosion. But if you still insist on a mustache, I recommend the Les Paul Solar Storm guitar strings. These can be inserted with a tennis shoe and a ligament tensor. But you have to really want it. Otherwise, there's nothing to believe in. You'll have to show me a sign. A sign that you're willing to take it to the limit. Across state lines into Beaverlick, Kentucky. I saw a mustache there once so huge it had a man under it. He made his living by milking snake venom. He made his peace with thoracic imaging in a gin-soaked masseuse parlor. Everyone called him Bill. But his real name was Gerardus Mercator. He made maps. And distorted things. He did this to make a better mailbox. A deep, resonant sound full of passion and pink stationary. His mustache was a gift from his face, which he wore everyday attending his life, a campaign he pursued with relish, and a counterfeit direction. He said latitude is all attitude. But if you don't know where you're going, you won't need a map. You'll need what you need. I don't know what you need. But you'll need it.

6:30 P.M. December 21st, 2022. The winter solstice. Earlier, around 1:00 P.M., Oriana and I decided to go for a walk. It was too intensely cold and icy to run. Going for a walk was the next best thing. I found the heaviest coat I could find, a pair of woolen gloves and a wool hat. Oriana dressed similarly, though she had a new wool hat with two flaps that covered her ears and part of her face. We loaded four sandwich bags with unsalted peanuts, two for me and two for Oriana, to feed the crows. They must be famished. Oriana had already taken a walk to the top of the hill to feed Louise, the lame crow with a completely useless leg that we've been feeding for four or five years. I remember feeding her on a cold rainy day last December and she sat high on a telephone wire and wouldn't come down. I found this puzzling. Was she meditating? Doing penance? Was this a purifying ritual? I don't understand crows. They're even more mysterious than cats.

It was bitter cold. As soon as I stepped outside, it was like getting punched. Our faces burned. I wished I'd had the foresight to bring a scarf. I envied Oriana's hat. I was tempted to turn around and get my scarf. But we kept going. We'd already gone a distance. The streets were glazed with ice an inch thick. They were barely walkable. Yet there were people driving on them. There were cars on many of the side streets abandoned at weird angles with sometimes chunks of wood under the tires. People who'd made the attempt and lost control of their car. I marveled that anyone could be that foolhardy, that delusional, to think they could drive a car over this ice without chains. Where did they have to be so badly that they would hazard such risk? Groceries, maybe? I know what that's like. Back in the day, as a bachelor, to run out of ice cream, or wine. Grocery stores are not easily accessed here, and we lost the most convenient of the grocery stores atop our hill, a Safeway. It was easily the most popular, especially as it had surface parking. You didn't have to park in a garage with all those smells of exhaust fumes and dreary concrete surfaces. You could walk in sunshine to the door of the grocery and leave Jack Kerouac on the backseat of the car as shelves upon shelves of canned goods and produce greeted you. You could stroll right in, take a second to let your eyes adjust to the darkness relative to the golden sunshine outside, grab a cart and roll it down the aisles filling it with bread and potatoes and blueberries and Gouda. Cabbages reposing in balls of whirly convolution. Cauliflower like the blanched brains of old widows. All of it gone. A big hole in the ground. They're building a new store that will have seven floors of luxury suites above it. Plank flooring, stainless steel appliances, quartz countertops, washer and dryer. Maybe a gym or nail salon. And, no doubt, below all that luxury and convenience, a huge labyrinthine parking garage that spirals ever downward into darkness.

The ice was nearly impossible to negotiate. Dicey as can be. One nasty slide and it's goodbye elbow. Hello concussion. We fed a lot of crows. They were truly hungry. One came down on the street and slid on his feet and lost balance. That's a rare sight, to see a bird lose balance. But he didn't lose it entirely. Crows are nimble. I've seen the maneuvers they make in flight. Believe me, they know what they're doing, and they do it with stunning artistry.

The Olympics to the west stood out in high definition. Winter does this: everything seems doubly precise in outline and texture in the winter. It must have something to do with the air in lower temperatures. Heat turns it to blurrier, more softened, sfumato-like displays. Winter chisels the world into icicles and lines so purely delineated they seem like collisions. With what I don't know. Vagueness. It falls off a cliff. This is the hard raw world of rock and crampon. Mountains appear craggier, especially when they poke through an encumbrance of mist and clouds.

On a knoll of the Turtle Mountains overlooking the North Dakota prairie, is a modern-day functioning Stonehenge in which the setting sun at each solstice and equinox sends its rays through the narrow slit of a stone slab and casts a golden beam across the darkening ground. It's called Mystical Horizons. It was designed by my father, who passed away before it was built.

It's almost been a year since my younger brother passed away. He was the last of my family.

I like that word, *revenant*. In French, it means ghost, though more technically it means harking back or returning. The dead do leave remnants in our minds. They continue to live among us in this hazy, residual way, until the people that remember them die. The stronger the bond, the more vividly they continue to haunt us. The conversations continue. But everything has been pre-recorded. Spontaneity is gone. I'm never caught off guard. But the dialogue gets pretty stale.

The warmth of our apartment was voluptuous when we returned. No other word for it. Voluptuous.

My keys were still icy cold. Takes a while for metal to get warm. Thanks to the gloves, my hands were still fairly nimble. I could easily fish my keys out and inset it into the lock. I like that twist when the tumblers fall into place. Sound of our rubber soles shifting about on slate tile.

I call this body home. And it goes home. Home to me. I'm inside looking out. Eyes work by turning light into electrical signals. These travel from the optic nerve to the brain, where the signals are turned into images, shapes and shadows and men and women, horses and monkeys, parrots and roses, rope and steam and vermilion and lobster and French ochre. Sometimes I see things that don't exist. I call these things spirits and eidolons and tremble with their poetry. Somebody left just now maybe it was me. Am I still here? I shall write another sentence and find out. Sometimes when I cast a sentence into the world it finds a corresponding spirit. Our numbers grow. A communion forms, a loose network of souls peripheral to the general society and completely unofficial. If one of our observations drifts strangely and unnaturally into the mainstream, it causes upset. People are sensitive about their fictions and beliefs. There are tribes and cults. No single narratives that bond the population as a whole. The former institutions have lost people's trust. Eventually, this may all turn to mulch and fertilize a new culture of hominid bonding. If something of our shared inquiries endures, we may be judged by a whole new set of principles and percepts. We may be accused of being a little too conveniently detached. Of being aloof, of being ivory tower postmodernist dissemblers. Which is both true and untrue, like everything else in this puzzling, contradictory world. All that is required is a little attention. But I get it. It's hard to break ranks in a regimented society.

I've lived half of my life on paper. I've lived the other half on borrowed time. One day I hope to see Montmartre secede from planet Earth and become a theme park on Callisto. There's nothing I like better than to ride a Harley in outer space. It looks good on paper. It looks even better in outer space. Enough to confuse an ornithologist. Why should darkness be theological? Darkness is shapeless and therefore freely available as a bundled service. You can enjoy it in the dark or in a fancy hotel in Reykjavik. Dim the lights. Pour some wine. Hug someone near. Hug the darkness. It feels anonymous, like mountains. You can feel it in the shoulder. Two new wings.

quale [kwä-lay]: _Eng_ n. 1. A property (such as hardness) considered apart from things that have that property. 2. A property that is experienced as distinct from any source it may have in a physical object. _Ital._ pron.a. 1. Which, what. 2. Who. 3. Some. 4. As, just as.

❦